Chase paused, trying to brace himself for how she was going to react to the next thing he had to tell her.

"There was blood on the floor."

That caused her breath to shudder, and she staggered back. Maybe would have fallen if Chase hadn't caught her. He hooked his arm around her waist, putting them body to body again. Also giving him feelings he didn't want to have.

Lust.

Not an especially good time for it, but it always seemed to happen with April. Chase cursed it and wished there was some way in hell he could make himself immune to her.

THE MARSHAL'S JUSTICE

USA TODAY Bestselling Author

DELORES FOSSEN

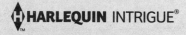

HARLEQUIN INTRIGUE®

Recycling programs
for this product may
not exist in your area.

ISBN-13: 978-0-373-69902-5

The Marshal's Justice

Copyright © 2016 by Delores Fossen

This edition published by arrangement with Harlequin Books S.A.

For questions and comments about the quality of this book, please contact us at CustomerService@Harlequin.com.

® and TM are trademarks of Harlequin Enterprises Limited or its corporate affiliates. Trademarks indicated with ® are registered in the United States Patent and Trademark Office, the Canadian Intellectual Property Office and in other countries.

Printed in U.S.A.

Delores Fossen, a *USA TODAY* bestselling author, has sold over fifty novels with millions of copies of her books in print worldwide. She's received a Booksellers' Best Award and an RT Reviewers' Choice Best Book Award. She was also a finalist for a prestigious RITA® Award. You can contact the author through her web page at deloresfossen.com.

Books by Delores Fossen

Harlequin Intrigue

Appaloosa Pass Ranch

Lone Wolf Lawman
Taking Aim at the Sheriff
Trouble with a Badge
The Marshal's Justice

Sweetwater Ranch

Maverick Sheriff
Cowboy Behind the Badge
Rustling Up Trouble
Kidnapping in Kendall County
The Deputy's Redemption
Reining in Justice
Surrendering to the Sheriff
A Lawman's Justice

HQN Books

The McCord Brothers

Texas on My Mind

Visit the Author Profile page
at Harlequin.com for more titles.

CAST OF CHARACTERS

Marshal Chase Crockett—When some WITSEC files are hacked, this tough cowboy cop learns that his former criminal informant and the mother of his newborn is now on the run with a team of hired guns after her. Despite the rift between the baby's mother and him, Chase has to risk everything to save them.

April Landis—A businesswoman turned criminal informant, she's been in WITSEC waiting to testify against a vicious cop-killer. April knows she's already turned Chase's life upside down, but she has no choice but to go to him and hope he can keep their precious baby out of the kidnapper's hands.

Bailey Crockett—Chase and April's newborn daughter who's caught in the middle of the danger.

Quentin Landis—April's no-good brother who's also in WITSEC. He could have been the one to put his sister, niece and Chase in the crosshairs of a killer.

Renée Edmunds—An heiress who might be mentally unstable. She's so obsessed with finding Quentin that she might have been the one to hack into WITSEC files.

Tony Crossman—Accused of killing a cop, he's in jail awaiting trial—a trial that won't happen if he can eliminate April and Quentin so they can't testify against him.

Malcolm Knox—He befriended April while she was in WITSEC, but is he the person he's claiming to be?

Chapter One

The shot cracked through the air. Mercy. That was definitely not what Marshal Chase Crockett wanted to hear.

Or see.

The bullet slammed into the woman he'd just spotted. Her gaze connected with Chase's a split second before she crumpled to the ground.

If she wasn't dead, she soon would be. Chase was sure of it.

He cursed when he couldn't go out in the clearing where she'd fallen and pull her out of the path of more gunfire. Cursed, too, that he hadn't been able to stop that bullet from hitting her in the first place.

How the devil had this happened?

He didn't have time to try to figure that out because the next bullet came right at him, and Chase had no choice but to dive behind a pile of rocks. Maybe he'd get a chance soon to return fire and make the shooter pay for what he had just done.

And what he'd done was shoot the criminal informant, Deanne McKinley, on the banks of Appaloosa Creek. A woman who had phoned Chase earlier and begged him to help her. If he'd just gotten her call a few minutes sooner, maybe he could have arrived in time to stop this.

Whatever *this* was.

Clearly, someone wanted Deanne dead, and now whoever had attacked her was shooting at Chase, too.

"If you want to get out of this alive, you might as well give up now," the gunman shouted.

Chase didn't recognize the voice, but he'd caught a glimpse of a guy wearing a ski mask before the man shot Deanne and then darted out of sight. He wasn't even sure if the idiot was yelling at him or Deanne. Chase didn't have nearly enough info, other than the call a half hour ago from Deanne to tell him she was in trouble. She said someone was trying to kill her, that she needed his help.

Help was exactly what Chase had intended to give her when he'd arrived.

So far, all he'd managed to do was dodge bullets, but if he had anything to say about that, things were about to change.

Chase heard Deanne's hoarse moan, and she moved her hand to her chest. *Alive.* He had to do something now to keep it that way.

He didn't know the exact location of the shooter, but Chase fired two shots in the guy's general direction. In the same motion, he scrambled toward Deanne to try to pull her away.

Basically, it was a high-risk move with little chance of succeeding.

Or at least it should have been.

But another set of shots blasted through the air. Definitely not ones that Chase or the gunman had fired. They'd come from a cluster of trees about thirty feet away, and the bullets had been aimed at the shooter.

Maybe backup had arrived a little sooner than Chase

had thought it would. Or it could be a hunter or nearby rancher who'd heard sounds of the attack and had come to help. Either way, he'd take it.

Chase grabbed hold of Deanne's arm and pulled her behind a tree. It wasn't much cover, but it was better than leaving her out in the open.

He fired off another shot to keep the gunman at bay and sent a quick text requesting an ambulance along with the backup. It would likely be one of his brothers who responded to his request since all three of them were in local law enforcement. Chase only hoped the backup and the ambulance arrived in time.

It'd be close.

Deanne was bleeding out from the gunshot she'd taken to the chest. Chase did his best to add some pressure to the wound, but it was hard to do that without constricting her breathing. He didn't want her to suffocate.

More shots came from the gunman.

The idiot was moving closer to them, no doubt coming in for the kill.

Deanne mumbled something, something that Chase didn't catch, and without taking his attention off the area where the shooter was positioned, he leaned in closer, hoping to hear what Deanne was trying to say.

"Help," Deanne whispered.

"Help is on the way," he assured her. Chase wanted to say how sorry he was for what had happened to her. Deanne had a criminal past, but she didn't deserve this.

Deanne shook her head. "No, help *her.*" Her gaze drifted in the direction where those two other shots had been fired.

Each word she spoke was a struggle, and by the time

she was done, Deanne was gasping for air. Still, she managed to say one last thing.

Something that twisted his stomach into a tight, hard knot.

No more breaths from Deanne. Her chest just stopped moving, and Chase could only watch the life drain from her eyes. Watch and mentally repeat what Deanne had said to him with her dying breath.

April's in trouble.

His gaze whipped in the direction of the second shooter. The person was still hidden behind a tree, but Chase had the sickening feeling that he knew who'd fired those two shots at the gunman.

Was April really out there?

Just the thought of it twisted and tightened that knot even more. There was plenty of bad blood between April and him. But a different kind of connection, too. One that would last a lifetime.

Because April was pregnant with Chase's baby.

However, April shouldn't be here. *Couldn't* be here. She was in WITSEC, tucked away somewhere safe with a new name and a location that even Chase didn't know. A necessary precaution so that no one could trace her by following him.

April was also nine months pregnant, ready to deliver any day now.

He waited until the original shooter fired another shot, and he used that to help him pinpoint the guy's position. Chase fired. He also got moving right away, heading toward those trees where the second shooter had been. Maybe he wouldn't find April there after all.

But if she was, then that meant something had gone wrong.

He tried to recall every word of the short phone conversation he'd had earlier with Deanne. She'd been frantic, said she was in her car, somewhere near the Appaloosa Creek Bridge, and that she was being tailed by a gunman wearing a ski mask.

Had Deanne said anything else?

No.

Definitely nothing about April being with her.

So, maybe he was wrong about April, and Deanne's words were merely the mumblings of a dying woman. And maybe that was one of his brothers out there helping him with the shots.

Chase scrambled his way through the trees and the underbrush, cursing the wet spring weather that'd clogged this part of the woods with mud and briars. It slowed him down.

He ducked behind a tree, fired off another shot and then had to reload. It was his last magazine so he'd have to be careful with the shots now and make every one count.

Whoever was returning fire at Deanne's killer didn't seem to have the problem of not enough ammunition. The person continued to shoot, spacing out the shots several seconds apart.

"Jericho?" Chase whispered, hoping his brother, the sheriff, was the one returning fire behind the sprawling oak that was now just a few yards away.

No answer.

And if it'd been Jericho, or his other brothers, Levi or Jax, they would have responded somehow to let him know not to fire in their direction.

Chase kept moving, working his way through the muck, and he finally got in position to spot someone. It was late afternoon and some sunlight still hung in the sky, but the woods created deep shadows. There was nowhere near enough light for him to see the person's face, but whoever it was wore all black.

He risked lifting his head just a little, to see how this shadowy figure would respond, but he or she didn't even seem to acknowledge Chase.

"I'm coming closer," Chase warned the person, hoping this didn't turn out to be a big mistake, and he scurried toward the tree.

Thank God the person didn't shoot him, but this definitely wasn't one of his brothers.

Not April, either.

Because while he still couldn't make out much of the person's face, he could see the silhouette of the body. Whoever this was darn sure wasn't nine months pregnant.

Chase scrambled the last few feet to the tree and landed on the ground right next to the person who was kneeling. His heart skipped a beat or two though when he saw the ski mask. Identical to the one worn by the other shooter.

Hell.

He brought up his gun. Took aim. Just as the person shoved up the ski mask to reveal her face.

April.

Yes, it was her, all right. There was no mistaking her now. The black hair, the wide blue eyes. But she didn't have her attention fixed on him. It was on the other shooter.

"Is Deanne okay?" she asked on a rise of breath.

"No. She's dead."

April had no reaction to that. Well, none that he could pick out in the dusky light anyway. A surprise. Deanne and she weren't friends. Far from it after everything that'd happened, but still April had to be shocked by a woman's murder.

However, reactions and that ski mask weren't his only concern about this situation. Chase couldn't stop himself from looking in the direction of her stomach again. Definitely flat.

"The baby?" he managed to say.

His baby. The one April should have been giving birth to any day now. But she certainly didn't have a newborn with her, and she didn't look as if she'd just delivered, either.

"Play along," she whispered, a split second before she hooked her left arm around his neck, dragged him in front of her and put her gun to his head.

"I have Marshal Crockett," April called out to someone.

"What the devil's going on here?" Chase snarled, and he shoved her away from him.

"You have to play along," April repeated. Definitely not the tone of a terrified woman on the run. Nor was that a weak grip she put on him when she yanked him back against her.

Damn. Was April up to her old tricks again?

"Put down your gun," she added in a whisper. "And whatever you do, don't shoot him."

Chase didn't get a chance to ask her anything else because he heard the footsteps. Heavy, hurried ones. And he soon spotted the guy who'd been firing shots at him.

The very snake who'd killed Deanne.

Chase didn't put down his gun as April had demanded, but she shoved his hand by his side. Maybe so that his weapon would be out of sight. Or perhaps because this was some kind of sick game she was playing.

The killer came right toward them, and the moment he spotted April—and the gun she had to Chase's head—he lifted his ski mask.

And he smiled.

Chase didn't recognize him. The guy was a stranger, but judging from his sheer size and the hardened look on his scarred face, this was a hired thug. He certainly didn't look like a man ready to negotiate surrender, not with that Kevlar vest and multiple guns holstered on his bulky body.

"Good job," the guy told April. "Well, sorta good. That wasn't you shooting at me, now, was it?"

"I aimed over your head. I wanted Marshal Crockett to think I was trying to kill you so he'd come to me. It worked."

Oh, man. Was this really a trap? Possibly. But Chase kept going back to April's *play along* comment.

What kind of sick plan was this?

The man stared at her. A long time. As if he might challenge what she'd just told him. Then, he shrugged. "Guess it did work. Now take a hike so I can finish this. Unless you'd rather watch while I have a word with your ex-lover. It might involve a bullet or two."

Shaking her head, April stood. Slowly. "No, I'd rather skip that part. Just give me what you promised, and I'll leave."

Chase stood, too, hoping it wasn't a mistake that he hadn't already put an end to this hulking clown. Or that he'd semi-trusted April when she'd rattled off those whispered instructions about not shooting the guy.

"Give me what you promised," April demanded to the man.

Now Chase heard some emotion in her voice. She was scared. Which meant whatever the heck was going on here was possibly about to take an even worse turn than it already had.

"You'll have to wait a little longer," the man said. He motioned for her to leave. "I'll meet you at your car, and you'll get it then."

Chase still didn't have a clue what this conversation was about, but he had no doubts that this bozo was about to try to kill him.

"You promised." April's voice was trembling now.

The man smiled again. There was no friendliness or humor in it. "And it's a promise I'll keep, okay? Just not right now at this second. I need to have that little chat with this cowboy cop first while you hurry along."

April stayed put, and even though Chase kept his attention on the man and couldn't see her, he thought she might be glaring at Deanne's killer. Chase was certainly doing his own share of glaring at both of them.

"I need you to find somebody in WITSEC," the killer told Chase. "April claimed she wasn't able to help, but since you're a marshal, I'm betting you got access to stuff that she doesn't. I need to find Quentin Landis."

Chase groaned. He shouldn't have been surprised this was about Quentin. It usually was when April was involved.

Because Quentin was her brother.

Along with being a criminal. And the only reason Chase had met April to begin with was because he'd been investigating Quentin. At the time he had thought

April was innocent and had no knowledge of her brother's criminal activity. He'd been dead wrong about that.

"You expect me just to tell you where he is?" Chase asked, making sure he let this jerk know that wasn't going to happen.

Quentin might be scum, but he was in WITSEC after turning state's evidence in an upcoming murder trial, and it was part of Chase's job to make sure that even scum stayed protected. Whether they deserved it or not.

The gunman stared at him. "Yeah. I didn't figure you'd cooperate, but we had to try, didn't we? Maybe if I put a few bullets in your kneecaps, you'll recall something."

"We?" Chase spared April a glance, but she only shook her head. He had no idea what that head shake meant.

Nor did he have time to figure it out.

"No!" April shouted. Not at Chase but at the gunman.

The gunman lifted his Glock and aimed it at Chase. Chase was doing the same to the killer with his own Smith & Wesson.

Chase beat him to it.

He didn't fire into the Kevlar vest, but instead he double-tapped two shots to the gunman's head. And Chase didn't miss. The man dropped like a sack of rocks just as Chase had intended.

With that taken care of, Chase turned to April. "Now, what the hell's going on?" he demanded.

But she didn't answer. Probably because of the hoarse sob that tore from her mouth. "Oh, God." And she kept repeating it.

She dropped to her knees and she grabbed the dead man by the shoulders, lifting his torso off the ground. "Tell me where she is!" April yelled. "Tell me." The sobbing got worse when she put her fingers to his neck. "He's dead. He can't be dead."

It wasn't exactly the reaction Chase had expected since she knew this snake was a killer and had been prepared to kill again.

She looked up at him, tears shimmering in her eyes. "The baby."

All right. That got his attention. "*Our* baby?" Chase asked.

April nodded, and her breath shattered. "Someone took her. And that dead man was my best hope at finding our daughter."

Chapter Two

April felt the fresh wave of panic slam into her like a Mack truck.

First the baby. Then Deanne's death. Now this.

The emotions were too raw and strong, overpowering her so much that they were hard to fight. But April knew she had no choice except to keep fighting.

If she gave in to it, her baby might be lost forever.

Despite possibly destroying evidence, April rifled through the dead man's pockets. Looking for anything that would tell her where he was holding the baby.

No wallet. No ID. No photos. No scraps of paper with details of any kind.

Nothing.

Tamping down the panic, she forced herself to get to her feet. Chase helped by taking hold of her arm. April didn't have to look at his expression to know that he wanted answers. And he wanted them *now*.

However, April didn't have some of those answers, especially the ones Chase would want most.

Even though Chase still had hold of her, April started toward Deanne. Yes, she knew the woman was dead. April had seen her fall after taking the bullet. Had also seen her talking with Chase moments before it looked as if she took her last breath. April didn't know what, or how much, Deanne had told him, but she figured she'd soon find out.

"Who has the baby?" he snapped. "And when was she taken?"

April had to shake her head again, and she motioned toward the dead man. "Whoever he was working for took her. Around midnight two masked gunmen broke into my house, held me at gunpoint and demanded to know where Quentin was. When I said I didn't know, they kidnapped the baby."

A sound came deep from within his chest. Not a good sound, either. Pure anger. "And you didn't call me?"

She'd braced herself for the question, and the anger. Or so she'd thought. Hard to brace herself, though, for that kind of emotion.

"The kidnapper said if I contacted you, anyone in your family or anyone in law enforcement, I'd never see the baby again." She hadn't wanted to believe that, but April hadn't been able to dismiss it, either. "They said they'd be in touch soon and left."

"So, you called Deanne instead." Chase didn't sound happy about that at all. Of course, nothing about this situation was going to make him happy.

"Yes, I thought it would be safe for her to come. I figured no one would be trailing Deanne to get to me. Especially after things ended so badly between us."

Well, it'd ended badly between Deanne and April's brother anyway. Deanne had been the one to turn Quentin in. Of course, in doing so Deanne had turned in April, as well.

"As a CI, Deanne dealt with dangerous thugs like the

ones who took the baby," April explained. "And she did come right away when I called her."

"Because she felt guilty for what happened," Chase supplied. "She shouldn't have. Both Quentin and you made your own beds."

Since it was true and there was no way to make Chase see the legal shades of gray that had gotten her to that point, April just continued with her explanation. "I waited for a ransom demand, or any kind of communication from the kidnappers. And about an hour and a half ago, someone finally called and said for me to come to the Appaloosa Creek Bridge, that there'd be instructions for getting the baby back."

Chase didn't come out and tell her she'd been stupid, but what he felt was written all over his face.

A face that shared a lot of features with their daughter.

Same light brown hair. Same deep blue eyes. It both broke April's heart and warmed it to see those features on her precious baby.

"I guess Deanne got spooked and called me?" Chase asked.

Chase was not going to like this, either. "Not quite. When I got to the bridge, the kidnapper was waiting for me. The same one you just killed. But he said he wouldn't give me the baby unless you came to the bridge, too. I tried to talk him out of that, but he insisted it was the only way."

She'd been right. Chase didn't like that. Because it meant she had lured him there.

"So, you had Deanne make the call," Chase said.

April nodded. "I knew if I called, you'd have too many questions, and I wouldn't have had time to get into it. Like now." She paused. "Are your brothers on the way?"

Chase didn't jump to respond, but he did follow her as she approached Deanne's body. "Yeah. They should be here any minute. How safe are we out here?" He took out his phone and fired off a text. To one of his brothers, no doubt, so they could find them in these woods.

"I'm not sure if it's safe at all," she admitted. "I'm sorry. I hadn't wanted to get you involved in this, but I didn't have a choice."

"You had choices. Everybody does."

They weren't just talking about the baby now but her past. A past that Chase was probably sorry had included him.

"Now tell me what the hell happened here," he insisted.

She would. But where to start? The past sixteen hours had been one nightmare after another. Though Chase would want to know the details prior to that. Especially one detail.

The baby.

The one they'd conceived nine months ago when they'd had to face yet another nightmare. Landing in bed with him had been a lapse in judgment. Or Chase would consider it a lapse, anyway. Yes, they'd been attracted to each other since they first met, but Chase considered her a common criminal. And in many ways, he was right.

"I gave birth two months early," she said.

April tried to rein in her emotions. The fear. The hatred for the person who'd put all of this in motion. Hard to rein in anything, though, when she knelt beside Deanne and touched her.

Dead.

Of course, she already knew that, but it sickened her to confirm it for herself. The tears came. No way to stop them, but she tried to brush them away. Later, she'd grieve for the woman who'd lost her life way too soon and had died trying to help April.

Later, April would do a lot of things.

After she figured out how to untangle this mess that could cost her the baby.

Chase knelt, too. So they were face-to-face. And even though he tossed some glares at her, he continued to keep watch around them.

Always the lawman.

A good lawman, too. For all the good it'd done. It hadn't been good enough to help Deanne or their daughter today.

"Why didn't you have someone call me and tell me you'd had the baby?" he snapped.

Yet another long story, and she was already dealing with too much to bring those memories this close to the surface. "Bailey…that's what I named her…was a preemie, and at first she had trouble breathing on her own. She had to spend most of the time since her birth in a neonatal unit. It was touch-and-go there for a while, but she's fine now."

At least April prayed she was.

And the possibility that she wasn't fine brought on the tears again. Sweet heaven, she was so tired of crying. So tired of being terrified. So tired of not having her precious baby in her arms.

"That doesn't explain why you didn't tell me." Chase's tone didn't soften despite the tears, but he finally cursed and slid his hand over her back. For a very brief moment. Probably in an attempt to comfort her.

Too bad it didn't work.

April figured she could use some serious comforting right now, but comfort wasn't going to help her find the baby.

"I didn't tell you at first because I didn't want to risk anyone following you to the hospital," she said. "Because I delivered so early, we didn't have nearly enough security in place for you to come running to me."

It was the truth. But it wouldn't be a truth that Chase wanted to hear. Soon, he'd press her for a better explanation.

But that had to wait.

"The gunman and I left our cars by the Appaloosa Creek Bridge," April told him. So that's the direction she headed. "Maybe there's something inside his car that'll help me find Bailey."

"Not me. *Us.* You're not looking for Bailey alone."

He hesitated when saying their daughter's name, the way someone would hesitate when pronouncing a foreign word. Maybe because he was just getting accustomed to the idea of fatherhood.

An idea that he'd struggled with for months.

Now, here it was, slugging him in the face. Crushing him, too. Because it was certainly crushing her.

"Maybe the baby is in the kidnapper's car?" Chase suggested.

"No. Believe me, I checked. I even looked in the trunk when he opened it to take out an extra gun and some ammo." There'd been absolutely no sign of the baby.

Chase walked in step beside her. "What about Deanne—was she faking being afraid so she could lure me here? Or was the gunman actually threatening to kill her then?

"Deanne's fear was real. And warranted. The thug said the only way I could get Bailey back was for you to come, and that if I didn't agree, he'd kill Deanne. I thought we'd be able to overpower him or something. I also didn't think he'd want you dead. Not right off the bat like that anyway."

She'd been wrong about a lot of things. Definitely a stupid plan.

"The thug made me put on these clothes," she said, motioning at the all-black garb. "Deanne, too. I'm not sure why exactly, but I think he wanted to make you believe you were surrounded by hired guns."

And the thug knew that Deanne and April couldn't just shoot him. Because he was the only one who knew the baby's location.

Still glaring, Chase cursed. Not general profanity, either. Like the glare, it was aimed specifically at her. But this time, the glare didn't last as long as the others. That's because Chase stopped and, without warning, latched on to her and hauled her behind a tree.

Had he heard something? Because she certainly hadn't. Of course, with her heartbeat thumping in her ears, it was hard to hear much of anything.

The moments crawled by, but Chase still didn't budge. "Why did that goon want to find Quentin?" he whispered. Obviously, he intended to use this waiting time to fill in some of the blanks. But in this case, she had just as many blanks as Chase did.

April had to shake her head. "My guess is Tony Crossman wants to settle up things with Quentin and me."

Which wasn't much of a guess at all because Quentin and she were responsible for putting the king of thugs, Tony Crossman, behind bars. Their testimony, along with the testimony of Crossman's CPA, had put the CPA, Quentin and April into WITSEC, too.

However, even behind bars Crossman still had plenty of money and resources, and he'd apparently used both to come after her and take the baby. There was only one thing that could have gotten her to cooperate with one of Crossman's thugs.

And that was Bailey.

"I haven't seen my brother the entire six months I've been in WITSEC," she added when Chase got them moving again.

Something Chase probably already knew because that'd been the plan all along. It would make it hard for Crossman's henchmen to find Quentin and her if they were in different places leading separate lives.

Chase mumbled more profanity. "Someone probably hacked into WITSEC files to find Bailey and you. We thought we had a breach not long ago, but it turned out to be a false alarm."

April had heard about that possible breach, and it'd involved yet someone else connected to Crossman. A criminal named Marcos Culver, who'd been running one of Crossman's side businesses of money laundering. But that man had never been a threat to her. And besides, Culver was dead now.

"I need to find out who could have hacked into WIT-SEC," Chase continued, "and try to link that person back to Crossman. Or anyone else who might be involved."

Even though he didn't spell it out, April knew what he meant. Chase believed her brother could be involved in this.

And maybe Quentin was.

After all, April would have paid a huge ransom to get Bailey back. Chase would have as well once he'd learned what had happened, and the one thing her brother probably needed right now was cash since he'd blown through his trust fund that their grandparents had set up for both of them. Still, something like this seemed extreme even for Quentin.

"Stop," Chase said, and without warning he yanked her behind another tree.

Again, April hadn't heard anything, but clearly he had because Chase lifted his head, listening. Finally, she heard the footsteps. Someone was coming up on them fast.

"Your brothers?" she whispered.

Chase shook his head.

April leaned out just a little and spotted the man skulking his way toward them. Definitely not a Crockett lawman. This guy was dressed all in black and was wearing a ski mask.

Another hired gun.

She instantly felt fear, and hope. This man could try to kill them, but he also might know something about Bailey.

Chase handed her his phone. "Text Jericho and give him the guy's position," he whispered. "Also tell Jericho we need him alive."

April couldn't do that fast enough. She certainly didn't want the sheriff eliminating this hired gun before they got a chance to talk to him.

Jericho didn't respond to the text, but April soon realized why. She saw him, and he wasn't that far behind the guy in the ski mask.

Her heart went to her knees.

April nearly shouted out for Jericho not to shoot the man, something that would have almost certainly put

Jericho in danger because it would have alerted the gunman. But Chase glanced down at her, shook his head.

"If Jericho had wanted this guy dead, he already would be," Chase mouthed.

It took her a moment to fight through the panic going on in her head, and April realized he was right. The man obviously didn't know that Jericho was tracking him, and she was well aware that the sheriff had a deadly aim.

Chase eased her even farther behind the tree so that her face and body were pressed right against the rough bark. Chase pressed, too. His chest against her back. Touching her. Of course, he hadn't meant for this to be an intimate situation, but it always seemed to be just that when she was within a hundred feet of Chase.

Her mind tried to shut out the memories. But her body remembered every second she'd spent in Chase's arms.

In his bed, too.

She could no longer see the gunman or Jericho, but April could still hear the footsteps. The guy wasn't moving that fast, but he was definitely headed right for them.

Did he know Chase and she were there?

Or like them was he simply trying to make his way to the car?

April hadn't seen a second gunman in the car that'd been left by the bridge, but it was possible he came in another vehicle. Not exactly a comforting thought.

Because Chase was pressed against her, April felt his muscles tense even more than they already were. He was getting ready for something.

But what exactly?

She soon got an answer to that, too. Chase lunged out

from cover, tackling the gunman, and he slammed the guy to the ground.

The gunman cursed, and he tried to bring up his weapon, no doubt to shoot Chase. But Chase didn't give him a chance to do that. He knocked the gun from the thug's hand.

That wasn't the end of the fight, though.

The guy punched Chase. Hard enough to have knocked the breath out of him, but Chase managed to deliver a punch of his own.

And just like that, the guy stopped fighting.

It took her a couple of seconds to spot Jericho. He was moving in and had a Glock aimed right at the gunman's head. April prayed the man wouldn't give Jericho a reason to pull the trigger.

"Where's the baby?" Chase demanded, pointing his gun at the man, too.

Jericho didn't make a sound, but April knew he had to be confused about his brother's question. Then, Jericho's gaze dropped to her stomach for a split second, and that seemed to tell him all he needed to know. The baby had been born.

And had been taken.

Later, Jericho would have as many questions as Chase and the rest of the Crocketts would. For now, though, this ski-masked man might tell her what she needed to know.

"Where is she?" April repeated.

He didn't answer. Chase yanked off the guy's mask, and like their other attacker, he wasn't someone she recognized.

Chase got right in his face with the gun. "I won't kill

you, but I'll make you wish you were dead if you don't tell me where the baby is."

When the man still stayed silent, Chase bashed his gun against the side of the guy's head. "Tell me!" Chase demanded.

The man didn't open his mouth, not until Chase drew back the gun again to hit him. "I don't know where she is. Somewhere with the nanny."

So her baby wasn't alone in these woods. That was something at least. Well, it was if this snake was telling the truth.

"A nanny you hired?" Chase asked her.

"No." Which meant it was someone working for the same person as these hired thugs.

"And where's the nanny?" April pressed, moving even closer to the gunman.

"Don't know. I don't!" he shouted when Chase made a move to hit him again. "She was in a separate car with the kid. A black four-door, and she was supposed to follow us here."

Chase glanced at his brother. That was all it took, just a glance. "I'll tell Jax to look for the car," Jericho volunteered.

With that search started, Chase turned back to the man. "Who's *us*? Who else is here?"

The man tipped his head to the dead guy. "Just Hank and me."

April wished she had a lie detector to know if he was telling the truth about there being no other gunmen, but even if he wasn't, that wouldn't stop her. "I'm going to look for the nanny's car," she said to no one in particular.

But Chase clearly thought she'd been talking to him

because he stopped her. "Hold on a second and I'll go with you."

Chase turned his attention back to the man and he put his gun in the guy's face. "One more question, and trust me, a wrong answer will cause you a lot of pain. Who hired you to do this?"

The guy's eyes widened, filling with fear. "I don't know. I swear, that's the truth. I just had orders to find anything that would lead to Quentin Landis. And to get that info by any means necessary. That includes killing you."

"Tony Crossman hired him," Jericho spat out. "Unless somebody else is gunning for you and your idiot brother." He slid a glare at April.

"I can't speak for Quentin, but I think only Crossman and you hate me," she settled for saying.

However, she wasn't sure at all that it was the truth.

Chase glanced at her, too, but his attention quickly shifted back to the gunman on the ground. He stared at him, his gun still poised to do some damage, but after several long moments, Chase stepped back.

"Arrest him," Chase said to his brother. "Maybe he'll remember some things in interrogation."

Jericho didn't waste any time hauling the man to his feet, and he took out some plastic cuffs from his pocket to restrain him.

"Go ahead," Jericho said as he checked the guy for other weapons. "Look for the nanny. I'll take care of this piece of dirt and get someone out here for the woman's body and the dead guy."

The word *body* gave April another slam of grief. And guilt. But there wasn't anything she could do for

Deanne right now. Though she could do something to find her baby.

April turned and started in the direction of the Appaloosa Creek Bridge. She'd made it only a few steps when Chase's phone rang. He caught up with her, glancing down at the phone screen before he answered it.

"It's Jax," Chase relayed to her, and he put the call on speaker while they kept running.

"I found a black four-door car," Jax said. "It's on the east side of the road, less than a quarter mile from the bridge."

Good. The gunman had said the nanny was driving a vehicle like that. "Is the baby there?" April and Chase asked in unison.

Her stomach sank, though, when Jax hesitated.

"Chase," Jax finally said, "you need to get over here right now." And with that, Jax hung up.

Chapter Three

Chase batted aside some low-hanging tree branches and ran as fast as he could.

His thoughts and heart were racing, too. He wasn't sure what had put the alarm in Jax's voice or why his brother had hung up without an explanation, but with everything else that'd gone on the past hour, Chase figured it could be *bad*.

And it could involve his baby.

He hadn't had even a moment to come to terms with the fact that he was already a father. Of course, he'd known April's delivery date was approaching, but Chase had thought he had a little more time to deal with it.

Or rather more time to deal with his feelings for April.

His feelings for the baby were solid—he loved her, sight unseen, and would lay down his life to protect her.

April was a different matter.

Chase did indeed regret sleeping with her nine months ago. It'd been a mistake, one that had caused his family pain on top of pain.

Him, too.

However, he didn't regret the baby. Not for one second. His only regret when it came to Bailey was that he hadn't been there when she needed him to protect her.

He could partly blame April for that.

If April had just told him about Bailey, then maybe he could have put some more security measures in place.

Somehow, April kept up with his breakneck pace, and it occurred to him that he should at least ask her if it was okay for her to be doing this. After all, she'd had a baby two months ago. Maybe this was too much activity, too soon for her body. But since he figured he didn't stand a chance of talking her into slowing down, Chase just kept running.

Even though it was only a couple of minutes, it seemed to take a lifetime or two for them to reach the road. The bridge was just to their left, but Chase went right since that was the direction where Jax should be. He prayed his brother was okay and hadn't been hurt by yet another hired gun.

Maybe that wasn't the reason Jax had put such an abrupt end to the call. But something had certainly caused him to do that. Since Jax had just as much experience as Chase in law enforcement, it must have been something damn important.

"I don't see him," April said.

She sounded frantic. Looked it, too. Her eyes were wild. Her breath racing, and yet she didn't even pause. She kept running up the road until Chase pulled her back to the side.

"This could be an ambush of some kind," he reminded her.

Something he didn't want to consider, but his lawman's experience put it—and plenty of other bad possibilities—in the forefront of his mind. It could have been the reason Jax ended the call. Because Jax could have walked into a dangerous situation.

Chase didn't want April and him doing the same thing.

He made sure his gun was ready. Made sure April was behind him, too, and using the trees and brush for cover, Chase made his way east. About a quarter of a mile, Jax had said, and from Chase's calculations, that meant his brother and God knew who or what else were just around the curve ahead.

"This way," Chase told her, and he led April just a few yards off the road and back into the woods so they could thread their way to Jax without being out in the open.

Finally, he spotted his brother. Jax was literally in the middle of the road, his gun aimed at the car.

Oh, man.

Nothing could have held April back at that point. She raced out onto the road while Chase tried to keep himself between her and whatever had put Jax on full alert. Chase soon saw the cause.

A woman.

Tall, blonde and wearing a white maternity dress. She was mega pregnant with her back against the car.

And a .38 aimed at Jax.

His brother hadn't been harmed. For now. That was something at least, but this was definitely a volatile situation.

Was this the nanny? The car description certainly fit. But the baby was nowhere in sight.

"Don't come any closer," the pregnant woman warned them. Her hands were shaking. Not a good sign since she had her index finger on the trigger, and the way she was holding the gun told Chase that she didn't have a lot of experience with firearms. "I've already told the deputy here that if he shoots me, he won't find the baby."

April was trembling as well, and she lowered her gun

to her side. "Where is she? Where's Bailey?" The worry and fear practically drenched her voice.

"Safe, for now. Keep it that way and don't come closer."

Chase didn't move, but unlike April he didn't lower his gun. He couldn't shoot a pregnant woman, but she might not be so anxious to shoot Jax if she had two guns trained on her.

He craned his neck to try to get a look at the interior of the car, but with the tinted windows, he couldn't see much of anything. The engine was running, the windows all up, and since the woman was between them and the car, Chase figured he wasn't going to get a better look inside until he dealt with the situation right in front of him.

"What do you want from us?" Chase asked her.

"Money, a getaway vehicle," Jax provided. "And any information about Quentin's whereabouts."

"The last one is especially important," the woman said, tears springing to her eyes. "I have to find him." She slid her left hand over her belly. "He has to know he's about to be a father."

Good grief. So, she was connected to Quentin? And clearly this woman wasn't just any ordinary nanny.

"I'm Quentin's sister," April said, taking a step toward her. "He wouldn't want you to hurt his niece. He wouldn't want any of this to be happening."

That was probably true. Quentin could be scum, but to the best of Chase's knowledge, the man had never endangered a baby.

"Quentin would want *me* protected. He wants to be with me and our baby, but he can't be because of him." The woman pointed at Chase. "You're the marshal who put him in WITSEC. You're the one who took Quentin away from me."

Obviously, she had a skewed idea of what'd happened six months ago. "I did that for his own safety."

"Then you can put me there with him! Quentin loves me and wants to be with me."

Since Quentin hadn't requested that and since this was the first Chase was hearing about the man having a pregnant girlfriend, he glanced at April to see if she'd known.

April shook her head. "I've never met her. But maybe Quentin mentioned your name," she added to the woman.

"I'm Renée Edmunds," she volunteered.

"Quentin didn't always tell me the details of his personal life," April mumbled. "He certainly didn't tell me he was about to become a father."

"Because he doesn't trust you, that's why," Renée snapped. "He said I wasn't to trust you because you betrayed him by spying on him. You became a criminal informant to save your own skin."

April nodded, readily admitting that. "Quentin was involved in some bad things then. With a very bad man. I did what I had to do to put an end to it."

That was the sanitized version anyway, and that very bad man was none other than Tony Crossman. April had uncovered her brother's illegal activity but had sat on it for a while. Long enough for someone to get killed. Only afterward had April turned CI to help arrest Crossman.

"Were you doing what you had to do when you slept with Quentin's enemy, Marshal Crockett?" Renée asked.

Quentin would indeed consider him his enemy. Chase felt the same way about him.

"Is that why you took our daughter, because you

thought it would help you find Quentin?" April went another step closer to Renée.

"I didn't take her." A hoarse sob tore from Renée's mouth, and she repeated her denial. "But when I got the call to be involved in this, I didn't say no. I'd do anything to see Quentin again."

Anything, including putting an innocent baby in danger. It didn't matter if Renée had or hadn't been the person who kidnapped Bailey, she certainly hadn't turned the baby over to the authorities. And she darn sure wasn't cooperating now.

Somehow, he had to get that gun out of her shaky hands.

"Who hired you?" Chase asked her, and he made sure he sounded like the lawman that he was. Maybe he could intimidate her into surrendering the weapon.

"I don't know," Renée said.

Chase huffed, already tired of this ordeal. He wanted it to end so he could find his daughter and deal with the aftermath of everything else going on here.

"Who hired *you*?" he tried again.

"I don't know!" Renée's answer was louder this time. "I got a call from a man who said Quentin was in danger and that if I wanted to find him then he'd help me."

"Did this man have a name?" Jax asked. He, too, sounded like a lawman. A riled one. Probably because he was as fed up with Quentin and April as Chase was. Still, his brother would do whatever it took to get the baby back.

"His name is Jason Toth," Renée finally answered. "He said he was Quentin's friend."

It wasn't a name Chase recognized, and apparently neither did April or Jax. Of course, whoever had come up with this sick plan probably wouldn't have used a real name.

"Do you know Tony Crossman?" Chase asked the woman.

She gave a shaky nod. "He's the man Quentin helped send to jail. He wants to hurt Quentin."

"Crossman wants to *kill* him," Chase spelled out for her. "And he'd do anything—that includes using you— to find him."

Chase didn't add more. He just waited and let Renée fill in the blanks. It didn't take her long.

"Toth might be working for Crossman," Renée whispered, her mouth trembling now.

Bingo. "I don't know Quentin's location," Chase continued, "but if I did and I told you, then Crossman could get to Quentin before you do. Let me guess, you're wearing some kind of wire right now so Toth can hear whatever you're saying?"

Renée's gaze drifted down toward her stomach. And she nodded. It was a good thing Chase hadn't known Quentin's whereabouts and revealed it because assassins would have likely already been on their way to kill him.

April cursed and stormed toward Renée. "Where's my baby?" she yelled to the person on the other end of that listening device.

April probably would have latched on to Renée as well, but Chase held her back. After all, Renée still had the gun, and the woman was past the point of just being panicked and upset. There was no telling what she would do in her state of mind.

"You need to come with us to the Appaloosa Pass sheriff's office," Chase told Renée. "We can figure out where the baby is. And just how much Crossman's henchman has learned." If anything. "You might be able to save Quentin from being hurt."

Chase didn't care a flying fig if Quentin got hurt. The only thing he wanted right now was the location of the baby. Once Bailey was safe, then he could deal with Crossman, his hired guns and anyone else who had a part in this.

"Oh, God," Renée said, tears spilling down her cheek. "I was a fool to trust Toth."

Yeah, she was. But Chase kept that to himself. "Just put down the gun and come with us."

She volleyed glances at the .38, Chase and April. When Renée lifted her hand, Chase was certain that she was about to surrender.

He was wrong.

Renée made a feral sound that came deep from within her throat. Definitely not the sound of a woman who'd just realized she'd made a huge mistake. This was more the sound a trapped animal would make.

She turned, racing around the back of the car. Chase still wasn't sure what she had in mind, but he didn't want to risk firing a warning shot. He cursed and went after her.

Renée didn't stop at the back of the car. She kept running. She jumped the narrow ditch and headed for the woods. For a pregnant woman, she ran pretty darn fast.

"Don't hurt your baby," April shouted out to her.

It was a good thing to say. It should have gotten a concerned, expectant mother to slow down.

But Renée definitely didn't slow down.

"She can't get away," April said, following right along behind Chase and the woman.

"Go after her," Jax insisted. "I'll stay and search the car to make sure there's no other gunman inside."

Good plan. Too bad Chase didn't have time to talk April into staying with Jax because she, too, went after Renée. Thankfully, it didn't take them long to catch up with the woman, and when they did, Chase latched on to her shoulder and dragged her to a stop.

Renée didn't exactly cooperate.

"Let me go," she shouted, and she started to fight. Clawing and scratching at Chase while she tried to kick him.

Chase did something about that .38. He knocked it from her hand and April snatched it up before Renée could grab it.

That still didn't stop Renée.

She rammed into Chase and she didn't hold back. Renée off-balanced them, and Chase knew he couldn't stop them from falling to the ground. However, he did try to take the brunt of the fall so that Renée's unborn baby wouldn't be hurt.

But when he heard April gasp, Chase figured he hadn't succeeded in doing that.

Until he saw what'd captured April's attention.

Renée's dress had been shoved up during the scuffle. Way up. Chase saw a wire, but he also saw something strapped to her stomach.

A fake baby bump.

"She's not even pregnant," April mumbled.

That caused Renée to make another of those feral sounds, and she started fighting again. Not just scratching and shoving this time, but she punched Chase hard in the face.

Enough of this.

Since he was no longer dealing with a pregnant woman, Chase rammed her against the ground and pinned her in place.

"Tell Jax I need a pair of plastic cuffs," Chase told April.

April turned, no doubt to call out to Jax. But his brother responded before she could even get out a word.

"Get up here now," Jax shouted. "I found a baby."

Chapter Four

April ran as fast as she could, the horrible thoughts running right along with her. Jax had said he'd found a baby, but that didn't mean it was Bailey, and it didn't mean her precious daughter was safe.

After all, the men who'd taken Bailey were the same ones who'd murdered Deanne.

Chase ran, too, dragging Renée along with him. But Renée still wasn't cooperating, and that slowed Chase down.

April finally reached the road, but her heart sank when she didn't see Jax. She soon spotted him, though. He was sitting in the backseat of the car next to an infant seat.

And Bailey was in that seat.

"She's okay," Jax insisted. "Someone's obviously been taking good care of her."

April's breath whooshed out, and she practically crawled over Jax to get to the baby. He stepped out, hurrying toward Chase so he could take hold of Renée. But Jax did more than that. He clamped his hand over Renée's mouth.

"I don't want her calling out for help if she's got any other comrades in the area," Jax said.

Yes, and it was something that April should have

thought about already. Renée could still be dangerous, but before April could deal with her, she had to see to Bailey first.

Bailey didn't appear to have any injuries, but April had to check for herself. She took her from the seat, peeling back the blanket so she could check for any scrapes or bruises. None.

Jax had been right. Someone had been taking care of her. Bailey had on a fresh diaper, a clean pink gown, and judging from the bottles in the diaper bag next to the infant seat, she'd been well fed. Thank God. She was okay.

But Chase wasn't.

April had been so caught up in making sure Bailey was unharmed that she hadn't noticed Chase was right there by the door, and he had his attention fixed on the baby. He looked as if someone had slugged him, but the shock lasted for only a couple of seconds. Then, April saw something else she instantly recognized.

Love.

One look at his daughter and Chase was as smitten as April was.

"They didn't hurt her," Chase said, gulping in a long breath.

The love was mixed with a hefty dose of relief. Again, that love and relief didn't extend to April. Chase's gaze was practically icy when it landed on her.

"You should have told me when she was born," Chase snarled and likely would have said a whole lot more if Jax hadn't cleared his throat to get their attention.

"I hate to break up this family reunion, but it's not a good idea for us to be hanging around out here. There could be other gunmen."

Jax was right. Plus, he was still dealing with Renée.

He kept his hand clamped over her mouth so she couldn't yell, but she was struggling to break free.

Chase glanced around, probably trying to keep watch and figure out a solution to this. "Don't say anything about where we're going," April reminded him. "Renée's wearing that wire."

"I disconnected it, but it's still taped to her fake baby bump."

Good. Because April didn't want any more info relayed back to whoever had hired the woman or any other of those thugs.

"Where are you parked?" Chase asked Jax.

Jax tipped his head toward the road. "I left the cruiser about a quarter of a mile from here."

Not that far, but he would have to fight Renée every step of the way. Chase obviously figured that out right away because he opened the driver's side door of the black car and got in.

"I'll drive you to the cruiser, and I can come back later and get my own car," he told Jax. "You and Renée get in the front. April can ride with Bailey in the back."

Good, because April didn't want Bailey next to the woman. At best, Renée seemed unstable, but she could also be a hired killer. How the heck had Quentin gotten involved with her?

Or maybe he hadn't.

April wasn't sure anything coming out of Renée's mouth had been the truth, but maybe they could sort it all out at the sheriff's office. It was possible they'd also get some info from the wire she was wearing. First, though, April needed to try to sort out things with Chase. Or rather make peace with him.

"Let me go!" Renée snarled again when Jax put her in the cruiser. "I want to talk to Quentin."

"Take a number," Chase muttered under his breath.

April wanted to talk to her brother as well, but she wasn't sure if he'd actually played a role in this. This had Crossman written all over it.

"Crossman must have hired someone to hack into WITSEC files to find me," April said, thinking out loud.

Chase met her gaze in the rearview mirror. "Then why didn't the hacking include Quentin? If Crossman found you yesterday, he could have found your brother, too, and he wouldn't have needed to use Renée."

True, and she definitely hadn't heard anything from the marshals about Quentin being injured or killed. Of course, perhaps they didn't know yet. That didn't help the throbbing in her chest.

April forced herself to think this through. "Maybe the hacker did get Quentin's file, but it's possible he's not staying at the place the marshals arranged for him. He's not exactly a rule follower."

Since Chase had known Quentin for two years, as long as he'd known her, there was no way he could argue with that. Plus, Chase and plenty of other lawmen had investigated Quentin. For a good reason, too. The bar her brother owned was a hangout for all sorts of criminals.

At one time, that included Tony Crossman himself.

And yes, Quentin had gotten involved with Crossman's schemes and had in turn gotten her involved since April handled the finances for him. Worse, Quentin had tricked her into helping Crossma n with some money laundering. Chase would never believe it was a dupe, though. No. He would always think she'd done it willingly.

In a way, she had.

Chase pulled to a stop behind the cruiser, and Jax didn't waste any time getting Renée out of the car. "Tell Quentin I need to see him right away," the woman shouted.

"Oh, I will," Chase assured her. He glanced back at April. "I'll deal with your brother soon."

April had no trouble hearing the implied threat— Chase would do that after he dealt with her. He didn't use the rearview mirror this time. Chase turned and looked at her. Despite the horrible circumstances, April still wasn't immune to that face. *Hot* seemed like much too mild a word when it came to Chase. He'd gotten to her from the first time they met. Was still getting to her.

But she forced that heat aside.

It was easy to do when his gaze went from her to Bailey. He couldn't actually see Bailey's face because of the rear-facing infant seat, but his expression softened a bit. Well, for a few seconds anyway. It would no doubt take him a while to come to terms with the realization that he was the father of a two-month-old baby.

"I need to call the marshals first," he said, taking out his phone. "They should check on Crossman's former CPA to make sure her identity hasn't been compromised, too."

That was a good idea, especially since it'd been the CPA, Jasmine Bronson, who'd been the one who'd actually witnessed Crossman talking about the murder he'd committed.

"After I'm done with the call," Chase added, "I want to hear everything. And I mean *everything*."

"Just be careful what you say when you make that call. The breach in security could have happened right there in that office."

He didn't dispute that, though it looked as if that's exactly what he wanted to do. Chase made the call to his boss, and he asked him to check to see if April's identity, or anyone else's, had been compromised.

"Start talking," Chase insisted the moment he finished the call. He didn't have his attention on April now. He was watching as Jax maneuvered Renée into the backseat of the cruiser. "You'd better have a darn good reason for keeping Bailey from me for even a minute much less two months. And I'm not buying your excuse that you gave me earlier about those thugs finding you through me."

"It wasn't an excuse." April took a deep breath before she continued. "The morning I went into labor, I got a call from Deanne, and she said she'd heard on the streets that someone was watching you with the hopes of finding me. Needless to say, I believe the person behind that was Crossman."

Chase immediately shook his head, and he drove away once Jax had everything under control with Renée. "I didn't see anyone watching me, and I would have noticed something like that."

Yes, he would have. Especially in the past couple of months. He would have been on high alert because of Bailey's impending birth and because he'd also been recently attacked by a serial killer. April didn't know the details of the attack, but she was betting Chase had been looking over his shoulder a lot.

"Deanne said she'd heard the watching was being done through cameras," April explained, "that someone had managed to set them up in or near your house and by the marshals' office. The CI also told her that there was an informant in the marshals' office, too.

"And you believed Deanne?" he snapped. He took the road toward the town of Appaloosa Pass.

"Why wouldn't I? Deanne's never lied to me. She was trying to help me tonight, and that's why she's dead." That caused her chest to tighten, and April had to fight back a fresh batch of tears.

"Jericho has the guy who was working with Deanne's killer in custody. We'll get justice for her," Chase reminded her. No doubt to get her mind back on their conversation.

"Yes, but justice won't bring her back."

"No," Chase quietly agreed. Maybe he was grieving some, too. After all, Deanne had been one of his own criminal informants for several years. "Who told Deanne I was being watched?"

"I have no idea. As you know, Deanne didn't like to share the names of her sources. She said it kept them cooperating so she could use them to get info to help the cops."

Chase made a grunt of agreement, and while continuing to keep watch, he pulled out his phone. "I need a big favor," he said to the person who answered. "When you get a chance, go to my place and see if anyone has put any surveillance cameras around the house. Call me if you find anything."

As he put his phone away, he said, "That was Teddy McQueen, one of the ranch hands. If he doesn't find anything, I'll have him go through the house itself."

A place she remembered well since it was where Bailey had been conceived.

April didn't have to tap too deeply into her memories to guess where someone would have planted a camera. There were several large shade trees in his yard, a detached garage and even a small barn. But with the hours that Chase put in as a marshal, it was indeed possible that someone had gotten inside the house.

"I couldn't be sure the person hadn't planted listening devices along with cameras," April explained.

That didn't soothe the glare Chase shot her. "So what? You weren't going to tell me at all?"

"I was, but Bailey didn't get out of the hospital until three days ago. I didn't want to call the marshals because of the possible informant."

"You could have sent Deanne to tell me."

"That was the plan. She didn't want to call you because she wasn't sure if the informant or one of Crossman's thugs had managed to tap your phone. And she did try to speak to you in person, but you weren't at the office."

"The Moonlight Strangler investigation," he grumbled several moments later.

Yes, *that*. A cause very close to home. Since Chase and his family had recently learned that a vicious serial killer, the Moonlight Strangler, was the biological father of Chase's adopted sister. The Moonlight Strangler had murdered Jax's wife and had even attacked Chase.

"I was out of the office a lot," Chase added along with some profanity. Probably beating himself up for not being there. But this wasn't his fault.

Again, it was Crossman's.

And that led April to her next concern when Chase took the final turn into town, and she spotted the sheriff's office.

"Is it safe for us to be here?" she asked.

Chase didn't exactly jump to answer that. "We won't be here long. I'll arrange for a safe house. Not through the marshals just in case Deanne was right about an informant. And we won't go to the ranch house or my place, either, just in case there are cameras set up."

Good. Chase's house was at the far edge of the ranch property, and with the threat of the cameras, she'd figured going there was out. However, she was glad he'd dismissed taking her to his family's home on the ranch. For one thing, it might not be safe there, either, and for another, she didn't want to have to face the rest of his family just yet.

Chase didn't pull into the parking lot. He stopped directly in front of the door of the sheriff's office and glanced around. Since it was only about six-thirty, there were still people out and about, and there were diners in the café across the street. Chase studied each one of them and made another call.

"Come to the front door," Chase said.

A moment later, Deputy Mack Parkman appeared in the doorway of the office. He was sporting a very concerned look, no doubt because he'd gotten updates from Jericho and knew they had a murder on their hands.

Mack's look of concern went up considerably when he saw the baby. Obviously, he'd known she was pregnant with Chase's child. Everyone in town knew. But like Chase, Mack hadn't known that she'd delivered.

"Don't bring in the infant seat," Chase warned her. He drew his gun and stepped out. "It could have a tracking device on it. Just take the baby and get out on the side near Mack. Once we're inside we can dispose of anything the baby's wearing in case it's bugged, too."

She hadn't even considered something like that, but thankfully Chase had. April eased the baby into her arms, bundling her in the blanket, and as Chase had instructed, she hurried inside. Chase followed, but they didn't stay in the reception area. He rushed her toward the hall and into Jericho's office.

"Jericho will be here any minute with the prisoner," Mack told them. "The ME is on the way to the woods for the bodies."

"Jax is on his way, too," Chase said. "He was right behind us and he'll have a prisoner with him, as well."

Mack nodded. "What do you need me to do?"

"We need baby supplies. Formula, bottles, clothes and a blanket. Have one of the clerks from the drugstore bring whatever they have. Also, the car outside and everything in it should be processed. I doubt there'll be anything inside to link it to Crossman, but we might get lucky."

"Crossman?" Mack's concern went up yet another notch. He belted out some profanity under his breath, then blushed when he glanced at the baby. "Sorry."

She waved off the apology because it wasn't necessary. Crossman was a killer. Worse, a cop killer.

And it was that murder that had put some blood on April's hands.

Mack stepped away, undoubtedly to take care of getting the CSIs out to examine the car and arrange for those supplies. Leaving Chase and her alone with the baby. The first moments they'd been together alone with Bailey.

Chase walked closer, staring down at her, and he touched his finger to Bailey's cheek. Bailey was half-asleep, but that got her attention, and she turned her head, studying Chase as hard as he was studying her.

The corner of Bailey's mouth lifted, and even though April figured it wasn't a real smile, it still had a powerful effect. Chase groaned, the impact of fatherhood no doubt hitting him hard. And hitting him in the exact same way it'd hit April. Because he smiled, too.

A rarity.

Chase Crockett wasn't exactly the smiling type—especially since things had fallen apart between them. Too bad because that smile stirred the too familiar heat inside April.

Heat she pushed aside again.

That was something she always had to do around Chase. Because he'd spent the past two years trying to put her brother behind bars, April and Chase had never dated. But that hadn't stopped them from landing in bed together. For one glorious night, Chase had been hers for the taking, but then his friend had been murdered. Crossman—and Quentin—had been implicated in that. And anything she'd ever hoped to have with Chase had vanished in the blink of an eye.

Well, everything except Bailey.

That would give them a connection that she was certain Chase would rather have with someone else. *Anyone* else.

"Check her for tracking devices," Chase prompted.

April hurried to do that, causing Bailey to fuss, but thankfully she didn't see anything on her gown, blanket or diaper. That was something at least.

She heard the front door open, and Chase stepped back into the hall. Even though she couldn't see who'd come in, she did notice the alarm on Chase's face.

"What's wrong?" Chase immediately asked.

April hurried to the door and looked out to see Jericho. He had the gunman in cuffs and handed him off to Mack, but his attention stayed on Chase.

"We've got trouble," Jericho answered. "Jax was attacked on the road. He's okay, but the woman he was bringing in just escaped."

Chapter Five

Chase so didn't want to have to deal with anything else right now. What he wanted to do was hold his daughter and get to know her. Instead, he was neck deep in making sure Crossman, or whoever was behind the kidnapping and attacks, didn't get to Bailey and April again.

That meant going to a safe house. Something he was still working on, but for now, his baby was stuck sleeping on the cot in the break room at the sheriff's office. Hardly premium accommodations, but Bailey didn't seem to mind. She was sacked out, not a care in the world. Unlike April.

Chase saw plenty of those *cares* in her eyes.

"Anything?" she asked the moment Chase stepped into the doorway of the break room. She moved away from the cot and came closer to him.

Chase figured that one-word question encompassed a lot because there were plenty of cogs moving in the investigation. What wasn't moving was a solution to put an end to this.

"Renée's still missing." Thanks to the help from a gunman who'd run Jax off the road and taken her.

April's mouth tightened, clearly not pleased about that. *Welcome to the club.*

Renée could have given them some answers, and now the woman was missing.

"And what about Jax? Is he really okay?" Not displeasure now but rather concern in April's voice.

Chase nodded. "A few cuts and bruises. He's pissed off more than anything." An emotion that Chase completely understood.

He should have made sure Jax wasn't being followed. Should have done more to protect his brother. But Chase had had so many things on his mind that he hadn't taken more precautions. That couldn't happen again. Because the next time, Jax or someone else could be killed.

April came even closer to him, glancing back at the baby. Probably to make sure their whispered conversation wasn't disturbing her. It wasn't. Now that Bailey had had a bottle, she was sleeping, well, like a baby. However, Chase was betting April and he wouldn't be getting much sleep, if any, tonight.

"I'm sorry," April said.

Not especially something Chase wanted to hear. Or feel. But he felt something all right.

Sympathy.

And he'd learned the hard way, that was never a good thing to feel when it came to April. Best to keep this conversation on a more business level. Easy to do since they had plenty of nonpersonal things to discuss.

Well, one huge thing anyway.

There was something he should probably tell her. Eventually. Something that was indeed personal. But it would have to wait.

"Someone did hack into WITSEC files," Chase confirmed. "We won't know the extent of what was compromised for a while, but it's obvious the hacker was able to find you."

"And my brother?" she asked.

"The marshals went to his house, but Quentin wasn't there. The place had been ransacked and there were signs of a struggle." Chase paused, trying to brace himself for how she was going to react to the next thing he had to tell her. "There was blood on the floor."

That caused her breath to shudder, and she staggered back. Maybe would have fallen if Chase hadn't caught her. He hooked his arm around her waist, putting them body to body again. Also giving him feelings he didn't want to have.

Lust.

Not an especially good time for it, but it always seemed to happen with April. Chase cursed it and wished there was some way in hell he could make himself immune to her.

Rather than stand there with her in his arms, Chase led her across the room and had her sit in one of the chairs at the dining table.

She shook her head. "Quentin doesn't even know how to get in touch with me if he needs help."

"No, but he knows how to contact me. If it's a real emergency, he'd call me."

April looked up at him, blinked. "You don't think the blood they found is real?"

Chase was 1,000 percent sure she wasn't going to like this. "I think it's real all right, but Quentin could have planted it so it would look as if he'd been injured. And he could have done that so we wouldn't believe he had any part in kidnapping Bailey."

There were holes in that particular theory, but Chase knew that Quentin was very good at doing criminal things.

"You think Quentin could have had Bailey kidnapped for ransom money," April said. She didn't exactly jump to deny that though it was no doubt what she wanted to do.

"It's possible. You have to admit your brother has been involved in some illegal moneymaking schemes before."

She didn't deny that, either. Couldn't. Because it'd been Quentin's dirty dealings with Crossman that had set this entire mess in motion.

"I don't think Quentin would work with Crossman," April said. "Not again. Not after what happened the last time."

And what'd happened the last time was murder. Specifically, the murder of a cop, Tina Murdock. Tina had gone to question Quentin, had found Crossman instead, and some kind of argument had ensued. Crossman had shot and killed her.

"You trust your brother a lot more than I do," Chase reminded her.

"I know. And I also know you don't trust me. That's all right. I deserve it."

She did. But there was no need for him to spell that out to her. April had known about her brother's illegal activity. If she had reported it sooner instead of trying to get Quentin out of hot water, Tina wouldn't have walked into the bar where she'd been murdered.

Of course, April hadn't mentioned anything about knowing of Tina's visit or her brother's criminal activity when she'd gone to Chase that night. Even though Chase hadn't known it at the time, she'd been looking for a shoulder to cry on because she was about to turn in her brother. And during the *consoling*, they'd landed in bed. Only afterward did Chase learn the truth, and he was still dealing with it.

"I need some good news," she said, groaning. "*Any* good news."

"The safe house will be ready soon. I didn't go through the marshals for it, just in case. Dexter Conway and one of the other deputies are setting up a place in the local area. They're stocking it now and making sure there's plenty of security. After we're settled there, I can work on getting you a new identity."

Just thinking about that put a knot in his gut. A knot that'd been there since he'd known April was pregnant with his child.

Basically, as long as Crossman was a threat, April and Bailey would have to live in hiding. And if he wanted to be part of his baby's life—which he absolutely did— Chase would have to go in hiding with them. It'd mean giving up everything he knew. His family. His job. His life.

But that's exactly what was going to happen.

Of course, Chase had thought he'd have a few more days to come to terms with it. However, the little girl sleeping on the cot was the ultimate reminder that his time as a marshal was nearly up.

And that crushed him.

Since April looked very tuned in to his thoughts and appeared to be on the verge of another apology, Chase nipped it in the bud and continued giving her the update on their situation.

"Teddy hasn't found any cameras or anything else suspicious at my place, but he'll keep looking," Chase explained. "And the marshals haven't discovered anyone in the office who could be a mole."

April kept staring at him. "You don't sound as if you think they'll actually find anything."

Chase shrugged. "Deanne could have been wrong."

"Maybe." April took a deep breath and repeated her noncommittal response. "But she believed she was right. Believed it enough to risk her life to help me find Bailey."

That put some tears back in her eyes, and this time April didn't succeed in blinking them away. "God, Chase, I got Deanne killed. That's more blood on my hands."

The tears came faster. Sobs, too. And he would have had to be a heartless jerk to just stand there and watch her fall apart. Chase sank down in the chair next to her and pulled her into his arms.

"You might have saved Tina, but Deanne's a different matter," he said. It wasn't exactly a full dose of comfort he was offering, but he hated the tears. Hated even more that there was reason for the crying. "It was Deanne's choice to try to help you. She was by the creek because she chose to be there."

And Chase was thankful for it. He hadn't wanted Deanne to die, but at least the woman had given up her life while trying to save Bailey.

"Please tell me the man who was working with Deanne's killer is talking," April said through the tears.

"Not talking exactly, but Jericho did learn some info about him when he took his prints. His name is Gene Rooks, and he's a career criminal. He lawyered up or rather a lawyer showed up here shortly after Jericho arrested Rooks."

She stayed quiet a moment, probably giving that some thought. "Someone must have been watching. That's how Crossman knew Rooks was in custody." Another pause. "If it's Crossman. Renée isn't off my suspect list just yet."

Nor his. It was obvious that Renée was desperate to find Quentin. Why exactly, Chase didn't know, but desperate people did stupid things.

"Is Renée Edmunds even her real name?" April asked.

Chase nodded. "I pulled up her DMV photo and it's a match. Unlike Rooks, Renée doesn't have a record. No family for us to contact, either. I've put out feelers to see if she has a genuine connection to your brother. She could be just a nutcase or a groupie."

There'd been plenty of publicity following Tina's murder and Crossman's arrest, and Quentin's photo had been plastered in the newspapers. Quentin was a rich, good-looking guy. A bad-boy criminal. He was the type who could have attracted a nut job. Including one who could have faked a pregnancy. Of course, it was just as possible that Renée had indeed had a relationship with Quentin, and that was something Chase would ask her.

If they found her, that is.

It was going to be hard to track her down. No job. Renée lived off a trust fund, and her neighbors said they hadn't seen her in weeks.

Chase's phone rang, and even though he'd lowered the sound, it still caused Bailey to stir. April sprang out of the chair to go to her while Chase glanced at the screen. It was Teddy McQueen, the ranch hand.

"I found something," Teddy said the moment Chase answered. "Two cameras. One on your front porch. The other on the back."

Chase choked back a groan because he didn't want to wake the baby, but that was not the news he wanted to hear. "You're sure?" he asked, stepping out into the hall.

However, he'd already gotten April's attention. Despite her having picked up the baby, she had her gaze fixed on Chase.

"Yeah, I'm sure," Teddy answered. "I didn't see them at first because someone had hidden them in the eaves. And that's not all I found. There are little black box–looking things—one underneath the windowsill in your office. There's a second one outside your bedroom."

Hell. Eavesdropping devices no doubt. It sickened him to think someone had trespassed onto Crockett land to do something like that. It sickened Chase even more that if April had indeed called him, then Crossman or whoever was behind this could have learned her and Bailey's whereabouts.

Of course, the person had learned it and kidnapped Bailey, but at least Chase hadn't been the one to spill that info.

But who had?

Chase intended to find out soon.

"You want me to take this stuff down?" Teddy asked.

"No. I'll need to call in the CSIs and have them do a clean sweep of the place." Because if the person had gotten close enough to install the cameras and bugs, the individual could have gotten inside, as well.

Chase thanked Teddy, ended the call and made another one to the CSI lab. The conversation was important, but Bailey snagged his attention. The baby was wide awake now and was smiling at April. Chase made the request for the sweep as quickly as he could and then joined them on the cot.

"Deanne was right," April said. Not exactly an *I told you so* tone. More like one of frustration. They were dealing with someone who was thorough and well connected. Definitely not a good combination.

Chase nodded and made a mental note to have the marshals look even harder for the possible mole in the office. Until then, he wouldn't make any calls to the marshals or share any information about April with them. Not exactly ideal because he would miss using their resources to help him figure out what was going on. But the mental note he was making flew right out his head when Bailey looked at him.

And she smiled.

Oh, man. That little smile packed a wallop.

"You okay?" April asked him.

He managed a nod but then got another wallop when April eased the baby into his arms. Chase had heard Jericho and Jax talk about what it felt like to be a father, but nothing had prepared him for this overwhelming love. It was instant and so strong that he was glad he was sitting or it would have brought him to his knees.

"I held my nephew when he was this age," Chase said. "This is different."

"Yes. And scary."

It was. Chase knew exactly what April meant. The stakes suddenly seemed sky-high. Because they were. Someone had already kidnapped Bailey once, and Chase had to make sure that his baby wasn't put in the path of any more danger.

"I didn't know if I could do this," he admitted. "If I could be a father," Chase clarified.

She nodded and most likely did understand. He'd made it clear to April so many times that he didn't consider himself daddy material. Chase had always thought he'd missed that particular Crockett gene.

Heck, maybe he had.

Just because he loved this baby, it didn't mean he'd be

a good father to her. Though he would try. Too bad trying might not be nearly enough. Suddenly, nothing seemed as if it'd be nearly enough.

Chase's gaze came to April's, and even though she didn't say a word, he saw the doubts in her eyes, too. Of course, she'd been telling him right from the start that his giving up his badge for fatherhood was a bad idea. That he would resent it. Maybe not this year. Or next. But eventually.

April wasn't completely wrong about that.

He wouldn't resent Bailey. Not ever. But Chase couldn't be sure that he would ever be able to get past what April had done. Not good. Because Bailey would eventually pick up on that.

"I want Bailey in my life," he said. "We'll just have to work out the rest as we go along."

April didn't get a chance to say anything about that because the footsteps got their attention. Jericho was walking up the hall toward them, and he had his phone pressed to his ear.

Chase put the baby back in April's arms and stood. Waiting for Jericho to finish his call. Thankfully, he didn't have to wait too long.

"That was Houston PD. A uniform was responding to a call in Quentin's neighborhood and spotted your brother near his house," Jericho explained.

April slowly got to her feet. "Is he okay?"

Jericho shook his head. "Quentin appeared to be bleeding, but he ran. The cop's in pursuit now."

Chapter Six

April held Bailey even though the baby was sound asleep and would likely stay that way for hours. Her head was spinning with too many bad thoughts and images. Ones that would be there for a lifetime no doubt.

Images of Deanne dead.

And of Bailey being ripped from April's arms during the kidnapping.

Having Bailey so close to her now helped stave off some of those nightmares. Being at the safe house helped some, too. But April still couldn't fight off all of those bad thoughts. Now she had her brother to worry about. The police had yet to find Quentin, and he was out there somewhere, on the run. Maybe injured.

Maybe dead.

Plus, there was the additional worry of being in the safe house itself. The place wasn't that big, only one living area, two bedrooms and two baths, and while it was better than staying at the sheriff's office, it meant close quarters. With Chase.

Chase finished up his latest round of calls. All whispered conversations he'd had in the kitchen. And while looking over the notes he'd taken during those calls, he made his way back into the living room. He checked

Bailey first, but it was obvious from Chase's bunched-up forehead that he'd learned some things in those conversations that hadn't pleased him.

"The CSIs gathered up all the cameras and bugs from my house," Chase explained, keeping his voice low probably so that he wouldn't wake the baby. "There were eight in all, and they'll be analyzed for prints and trace. We might get lucky."

She doubted Crossman's lackeys would be that careless, especially after they'd done such a thorough job of installing them. After all, Chase hadn't had a clue they were there until April had pointed out the possibility.

Chase scowled again, something he'd been doing all night, and despite what he'd just said to her, he looked at her as if she'd screwed up yet once again.

And in his eyes she had.

But since Deanne had been right about those cameras at Chase's place, the woman had probably been right about the mole in the marshals' office, as well. It'd been too big of a risk for April to call him when Bailey was born. Of course, in hindsight that hadn't kept Bailey safe. Maybe nothing would, and that broke April's heart.

"What about the man you killed, the one who murdered Deanne," she said. She kept her voice at a whisper, too. "Anything more on him?"

"Nothing. Especially nothing to connect us to Crossman or Deanne. I thought maybe Deanne knew him. Maybe they had somehow been involved."

He didn't need to spell that out. Chase had been looking to see if Deanne had been hired to lure Chase and her to that creek. "Deanne was just as afraid of Crossman as I am," April pointed out.

"Maybe. But Deanne had been living her normal life.

Well, normal for a CI anyway. If Crossman hadn't gone after her in these past six months, then I figured he didn't want to pay her back for the part she'd played in his arrest."

And Deanne had indeed played a part. But the difference was Deanne hadn't agreed to testify against Crossman. Instead, the cops had made a deal with April and Quentin because they thought their lack of a police record would make them more credible. They'd turned informant, and in exchange they wouldn't be prosecuted for the crimes that'd gone on in the bar that Quentin owned.

In Crossman's eyes, that no doubt made them traitors. Along with his CPA, who was also scheduled to testify at his upcoming trial.

"I want to pay for Deanne's funeral," April offered. "It's the least I can do for her."

Chase nodded. "I'll let Jericho know, but it'll be a while before the ME will release the body."

Yes, because it was a murder.

"Still no sign of Quentin," Chase continued a moment later, "but the blood found in his house is being tested to see if it's really his."

April had been in worst-case-scenario mode for a while now, and she hadn't figured the blood belonged to anyone but Quentin. However, maybe it belonged to one of Crossman's thugs. She hoped it did. Maybe Quentin had managed to hurt one of them before he'd escaped.

Chase looked over his notes. "I found out more about Renée. The local cops interviewed some of her neighbors, and according to several of them, she's mentally ill. Has been for years."

April groaned softly. This was the woman who'd had Bailey for hours. Thank God Renée hadn't done anything to harm her. "Did Renée's neighbors believe she was actually pregnant?"

"Yeah. With Quentin's baby." Chase paused. "I think we have to consider that Renée, not Crossman, was behind the kidnapping. It's possible she hired someone to hack into WITSEC to find you because she was planning to pass off Bailey as her and Quentin's child."

April's stomach twisted and turned to the point where she had to take several deep breaths to steady herself. "If that's true, then she hired those gunmen. She's the one responsible for Deanne's death."

Chase nodded. "And it could have been her plan to kill us once she found out where Quentin was."

What sickened April even more was that it could have worked. If Renée and Quentin had been actual lovers, that is. Since Quentin had many lovers, she figured Renée could be telling the truth about that.

"If Renée hired those two gunmen, then she could have hired others," April said, thinking out loud. "Or at least one other one who helped her escape."

He nodded. "That's what I was thinking, too. Even though Jax said Renée seemed scared when the gunman took her. Of course, she could have been faking that or maybe she decided hired thugs weren't so trustworthy after all."

True. The thugs could have turned on Renée.

"Renée has an estranged husband we're trying to track down," Chase added. "His name is Shane Hackett, and one of the neighbors said whenever Renée's in trouble, she always turns to Shane for help."

Well, that was a start. The woman was definitely in trouble now so maybe she was with her husband. Though

April couldn't imagine Shane or anyone else staying with a woman who was so obsessed with another man.

"Any indications that Shane knows about Renée's possible affair with Quentin?" she asked.

"He knows. That's the reason Renée and he separated. He hasn't filed for a divorce yet, though, and at least one neighbor thought that was because Shane was still in love with her."

Heaven help him. Of course, it was possible Shane was off his rocker, too.

"I can't get started on a more permanent safe house and a new WITSEC identity for the three of us," Chase continued a moment later. "Not until I'm sure it's okay to deal with the marshals. But we can stay here until I figure out a better solution."

Chase walked closer, eased down on the arm of the sofa next to her. No scowl this time because he looked at Bailey instead of her. He smiled, something he had been doing every time he looked at their daughter.

That smile could be trouble.

Not just because it stirred the heat inside April but because the love he had for Bailey might make it harder for her to talk him out of making one of the biggest mistakes of his life.

"You told me once you had no plans for fatherhood," April tossed out there. Obviously, not very subtle.

His eyebrow lifted, and Chase gave her a *where's this going?* look. "I didn't. That was then. This is now."

Yes, but his *now* was colored by the love he had for his daughter. "You said the badge would always be your first priority. What you loved most."

Oh, that got her another scowl. "What I love most is my family. That includes Bailey." He huffed. "What's this about? Are you trying to talk me out of going into WITSEC with you?"

"Yes," she readily answered. "Just hear me out," April added before he could dismiss her. "You do love being a marshal. You and your brothers have that whole need-to-get-justice thing. Nothing wrong with that, but it's not just a job. It's a way of life. It's *you*."

The scowl got worse. "If you think I'll just walk away from my daughter—"

"No, but I believe there's another way of being a father without giving up what you are. *Who* you are," April corrected. "It wouldn't be easy, but we could set up secure locations for you to visit Bailey on a regular basis."

"Visitation rights." Chase said that as if it were profanity. Somehow, though, despite the intense conversation, he managed to keep his voice soft. "I don't want to just visit my daughter. I want to be her father."

"I know. But I'm trying to look down the road. We might be in WITSEC for the rest of our lives. What will you do? Because you certainly can't be in law enforcement again. That'd make you too easy to track."

"So, I'll find something else."

She groaned. "And at some point, you could start to resent giving up your badge. You might not want to resent it, but you will."

"And you won't?" he fired back.

"It's different for me. I wasn't exactly looking to hang on to the life I had. Not after what happened."

April saw the moment that Chase shut down. The subject was straying too close to something he didn't want to discuss with her. Not now. Maybe not ever. The murder of the cop.

The one she could have prevented.

"Just think about it," April suggested.

Chase didn't have time to think about that though or anything else she'd said because his phone rang. It woke Bailey, and the baby started to fuss. However, even the fussing didn't stop April from seeing the puzzled look on Chase's face.

"You know anyone by the name of Melody Sutter-field?" he asked, glancing at his phone screen.

April had to shake her head, but she instantly had a bad thought about all of this. "Is there any way someone could use your phone to trace our location?"

"No." But Chase didn't answer the call until she had the bottle in Bailey's mouth to quiet her. He put the call on speaker, but he didn't say anything.

"Marshal Crockett," April heard the caller say. Not a woman as the caller ID had indicated. It was a man. One whose voice April instantly recognized.

The chill slammed through her. Head to toe. Chase mumbled some profanity. Because he obviously recognized the caller, too.

It was Tony Crossman.

"Cat got your tongue, Marshal?" Crossman taunted. "Or have you defriended me?"

"I seriously doubt you got permission for this call," Chase said. No taunting for him. His eyes narrowed. "Let me guess—you're using your lawyer's phone."

"Guilty. But I needed to talk to you, and this was the only way. I heard Deanne was dead."

"Who told you that?" Chase countered.

"I'm in jail, not deaf. It's on the news. And some-one hacked into WITSEC files." It wasn't a question. "You've had a rough night, Marshal. April and her scum-bag brother, too."

"Did you do something to my brother?" April snapped.

Obviously, Chase hadn't wanted her to say anything, but if Crossman was talking, she needed to hear what he had to say. Besides, Crossman had probably already figured out that Bailey and she would be with Chase.

"How could I do anything to Quentin?" Crossman challenged. "I'm behind bars. You know that better than anyone because you lied to put me here."

"No lies. In case you've developed selective amnesia, you should remember I found proof that you were using Quentin's bar to launder money."

"Yes, that. But yet you didn't go to the cops. Must not have thought I was doing anything so wrong if you didn't report it or confront me about it."

Despite the glare Chase was giving her, April continued. "I was trying to protect my brother. And gather more evidence against you. I didn't know you were going to gun down a cop."

Crossman made a noncommittal sound. "All that sneaking around on your part, trying to gather dirt on me. Then, you got distracted by the marshal. Things didn't work out so great between you, though, when he learned you knew all about a sister in blue being killed."

"A woman you killed," she pointed out.

"Allegedly."

"You're in jail, waiting to be tried for it," April reminded him. "Your CPA actually heard you talking about it. And I didn't know about the dead cop when I went to Chase."

"Allegedly," Crossman repeated. "That's the rift between you two, isn't it? Chase says you knew. You said you didn't. So what's really true?"

"Did you call for a specific reason?" Chase demanded before April could say anything else.

Crossman took his time answering. "I did. I wanted April to know I'm not behind this. I didn't hack into WITSEC and I didn't kill Deanne."

April rolled her eyes. "I'm just supposed to take your word for that?"

"Of course. Why would I lie?"

She could think of a very good reason. "Because it wouldn't look good if we managed to tack on more charges to the ones you're already facing, that's why." April wished she could see his face to know if she'd struck a nerve.

"Maybe. And maybe I'm trying to help you. For instance, you need to watch out for Malcolm Knox."

Everything inside her went still, and Chase looked at her, obviously wanting an explanation. Well, she wanted some explaining done, too.

"How do you know Malcolm?" she asked.

"I know lots about you and your new life. Be careful, April. Malcolm has some pretty nasty secrets of his own. Bye for now." Crossman hung up before April could ask about those secrets.

"Who's Malcolm?" Chase immediately wanted to know.

"Someone I met when Bailey was in the hospital. He's supposedly a cattle baron and was regularly visiting a sick friend."

Chase's stare stayed on her. "Supposedly? Does that mean you didn't believe him?"

"I didn't trust him. But then, I didn't trust anyone I came in contact with." She paused. "Truth is, he gave me the creeps. He kept showing up outside Bailey's room."

His eyebrow lifted. "Stalking you?"

She shrugged. "I did a background check on him and he doesn't have a record or any history of that. But maybe I need to do another check if Crossman's warning me about him."

"Crossman could be lying or yanking your chain," Chase reminded her. But then he groaned, scrubbed his hand over his face. "Or there's another possibility. Malcolm could be working for Crossman."

Mercy, that didn't help the sickening chill she was trying to stave off. Just hearing Crossman's voice had been bad enough, but if Malcolm did indeed work for him, then that meant Crossman had had "eyes" on her for two months. And one of his thugs had been way too close to Bailey that whole time.

"I'll ask Jericho to see what he can find out about Malcolm." Chase fired off a text to his brother.

April thanked him and tried to rein in her fear. Hard to do, though, with Crossman still a threat. Maybe Malcolm was one, too. Having Bailey in her arms helped some, but once again, April found herself fighting back tears.

Tears that caused Chase to scowl again.

"Sorry." April wiped them away as fast as she could. "The last thing you need right now is a crying woman. Especially a woman who's caused you nothing but trouble."

His gaze stayed fixed on her, and by degrees the scowl softened. Chase gave a heavy sigh, reached out and touched her arm. Not a hug, but it still gave her far more comfort than it should have.

"You've caused trouble, yes," he said, "but you don't deserve what's happening to you. Neither does Bailey."

No, her baby didn't deserve it. "I'm afraid this will

be her life. Hiding out in safe houses. Having to learn to look over her shoulder and not trusting anyone."

He nodded. "And that's why I need to go into WITSEC with you. I want to be able to protect her."

April couldn't argue with the protection part, but she prayed there would be another way. After all, Bailey wasn't the only family Chase had, and leaving his life would mean leaving them, too. And being with her. Something that would never sit well with him.

"It was true what I said to Crossman," she tossed out there. "I didn't know the cop had been killed when I went to your house that night, and I didn't go there expecting to land in bed with you. I went because I was upset and wanted to talk to you."

A muscle flickered in his jaw, and his gaze slowly came back to hers. "You didn't seduce me. I willingly got into that bed with you."

True, but even now she could see that he still regretted it. Despite Bailey, Chase always would, and that put the ache right back in her chest.

His phone rang again, and for a moment April thought it was Crossman calling back for another round of taunting. But it wasn't Crossman this time. It was Jericho. Chase answered it and put it on speaker.

"We found Quentin," Jericho said the moment he was on the line.

April felt the jolt of relief. Followed by another jolt of fear. Because that wasn't a good news kind of tone from Jericho.

"Quentin's in the Appaloosa Pass Hospital," Jericho explained. "He walked in and admitted himself about fifteen minutes ago."

"Is he all right?" April asked.

"He's hurt, a gunshot wound to the arm, but he'll live. He wants to see you now, but I told him that's not going to happen. Not until we have plenty of security in place."

"Why does he want to see April?" There was plenty of mistrust and skepticism in Chase's expression and voice.

"I'll tell you what he told me. You can decide if it's the truth or not. He won't spill anything to me, but Quentin claims he knows who's trying to kill April and you."

Chapter Seven

Chase figured visiting Quentin in the hospital wasn't a smart thing to do, but he'd also known right from the start that he stood no chance of nixing the idea. Despite the kidnapping, attack and the mess that Quentin had caused, April had every intention of seeing her brother.

But that didn't mean Chase was going to allow Bailey to be put in danger.

His brother Levi and Deputy Mack Parkman had come to the safe house to stay with the baby while Chase and April ventured into Appaloosa Pass to see Quentin. And they wouldn't make that visit alone. Jax was meeting them there. As far as Chase was concerned, he was treating Quentin just as he would any other dangerous criminal who crossed his path.

"It's not too late to change your mind," Chase said to April as he took the final turn toward town. "You can always call your brother and demand to know what information he has."

"He won't tell me unless I'm there," April insisted.

And to her credit, she had tried to get that info from Quentin over the phone. But Quentin had only restated his demand that she come to see him in person. Still,

Quentin might change his tune if April flat out refused—especially if he did indeed want to save her life.

However, Chase wasn't so sure that was the case. Quentin might not care if his sister was in danger. Especially since he'd already been hurt. Chase still didn't know the details of how Quentin had been shot, but it was one of the questions Chase intended to ask the man.

"I don't trust Quentin," she said, surprising him. She'd always been so defensive when it came to her kid brother. "But I want to see his face when he tells me what he wants me to hear."

Chase gave that some thought. "You think Quentin could have been involved in the kidnapping?"

"I don't want to believe it." She sighed, leaned her head against the truck window. "But he goes through money like water and he has a penchant for getting involved with the worst kind of people. I believe he could have gotten himself into some kind of bind and needs money desperately enough to have possibly done something like this. *Possibly*," April emphasized.

Chase had to admit it was a *possibly* for him, too. Quentin was a scumbag, no doubt about that, but Crossman and Renée were still their top suspects, with Crossman occupying the number one slot on that very short list.

His phone rang, causing April to practically snap to attention. No doubt because she was worried about something going wrong at the safe house. But it wasn't Levi or Mack. It was Jericho.

"I just got the background check on Malcolm Knox," Jericho said the moment Chase answered. Chase put the call on speaker since he knew this was something April would want to hear. "He's rich. Worth millions. He's a cattleman and also owns a very high-end security company. Thirty-nine and never been married. No criminal record, not even a parking ticket. So, you want to tell me why you needed a check on him?"

"Because Crossman warned April about him," Chase answered.

"And you believe Crossman?"

"No." Chase didn't even have to give that any thought. "But I want to know if there's a connection. It's possible Crossman used Malcolm to spy on April while she was in WITSEC."

April didn't nod exactly, but he saw the agreement in her eyes. And the chill that went through her. She'd said she hadn't exactly trusted Malcolm, but it had to make her sick to think that one of Crossman's henchmen could have been so close to her at such a vulnerable time.

"I didn't find any obvious connection to Crossman," Jericho said. "But there's something about this guy that's just not right. Perfect credit, perfect driving record. Hell, he even had a perfect grade point average in college. Everything in his background lines up in *perfect* detail."

Normally, a good clean record didn't bother Chase, but it did in this case. "You think he's living under a created identity?"

"Maybe. But if so, he's not in WITSEC, and he's not an undercover cop or in any other form of law enforcement that I can find. That means if he's living under a false identity, he's likely doing it for his own reasons."

And Chase figured those reasons probably weren't good ones. "Were you able to get his financials?"

"Some. Lots of money in and out of his accounts. Hard to tell if he's getting regular payouts from someone like Crossman. But I'll do some more digging."

"Thanks," Chase told him, and he took the final turn

to the hospital. "Anything new with the prisoner this morning?" Not that he expected Gene Rooks to start blabbing, but Chase could hope the man had had a change of heart.

"Nothing yet, but Rooks is with his lawyer now. And no, I can't trace the lawyer back to Crossman or Renée. Already tried." Jericho paused. "The lab called on that blood they found in Quentin's house. It wasn't his, and it's not a match to anybody in the system."

April shook her head. "But Quentin was shot."

"Not there at his place. Or if it was there, he didn't leave any blood behind. I questioned Quentin about his injury, but he's being very vague. If you get answers from him, I want to hear them."

"Of course. Any news about Renée?"

"She's still at large. Still nothing on those bugs and cameras the CSIs gathered from your house. There were no prints or trace on them, but they're trying to find the location where the images and recordings were being sent."

"They can do that?" Chase asked.

"They can try. Don't get your hopes up. I think our best bet at finding out who's behind this is to get what you can from Quentin."

Chase believed that as well, and he ended the call when he pulled into the hospital parking lot. He spotted Jax right away under the awning at the drop-off area, and Jax motioned for him to park right by the door. Good. Because Chase didn't want April out in the open any longer than necessary.

"How's Quentin?" April immediately asked him.

Jax didn't answer right away and didn't waste any time near the door. Firing glances all around, he got them moving out of the reception area and up the hall. "He's fine. The doc said he'll be released this afternoon."

April didn't seem relieved about that, and Chase knew why. Being released could mean Quentin would be in even more danger since they weren't sure yet if they could trust the marshals.

"Who'll be protecting him?" April pressed.

Jax seemed annoyed, not with the question exactly but with the answer. "Me. The other deputies weren't exactly jumping to volunteer."

Chase didn't blame them. Quentin had been business partners with a cop killer. That wouldn't put the man on any popularity lists with law enforcement.

"Thank you," April said as they made their way down the hall.

"No need for thanks. I'm hoping Quentin will lead us to some information about who kidnapped Bailey." Which meant Jax thought Quentin might have played a part in that, too.

Chase didn't have to guess which room Quentin was in because the uniformed hospital security guard was posted outside the door. He opened it for them, and Jax went in ahead of April. Probably to make sure the area was still safe. It was. Only Quentin was there, and he was in the bed hooked up to an IV.

April didn't rush toward him, but Chase did get her inside the room so he could shut the door. He could have sworn the temperature in the room dropped with the frosty looks April and Quentin were giving each other. Seeing that was a first for Chase. April had always jumped to defend her brother and had always acted like a mother hen whenever she was around him.

"I'm glad you came," Quentin greeted, his attention going straight to her stomach. "I heard you had the baby."

"Who told you?" she snapped.

Quentin's frost intensified. "It doesn't matter. I'm sorry someone tried to kidnap her."

"They didn't try. They succeeded. Chase and I just got her back last night." She glanced away from him. "Deanne's dead."

"Yes, I found out about that, too." Something flickered through Quentin's eyes. Grief maybe? Or it could be fake grief. "Who killed her?"

"We don't have an ID on him yet, but he was working with a man named Gene Rooks," Chase answered. "Do you know him?"

The icy look he'd given his sister was a drop in the bucket compared with the one Quentin gave Chase. "Are you accusing me of something?"

"I'm only asking a question. You have a guilty conscience?"

Quentin growled out some profanity under his breath. "No, I just know how you are. You've been on a vendetta to get me for years."

Chase tapped his badge. "Just doing my job. I'm funny like that."

His attempt at smart-mouthed humor didn't soften Quentin's glare one bit. And it wasn't moving this conversation in a direction it needed to go. "Did you have anything to do with the kidnapping and attack on April and me that took place yesterday?"

"Of course not. Why would you think such a thing?" The denial was loud and intense enough. But that didn't mean Chase was buying it.

"Because you could be broke enough to be desperate."

Quentin dodged his gaze. Definitely not a good sign. "I do need money, but there's no way I'd kidnap my own niece to get it."

The room went completely silent for several moments.

"How'd you even know I'd had the baby?" April asked, taking the question right out of Chase's mouth. "And while you're explaining that, tell us how you found out about the kidnapping and that Deanne was dead."

Quentin huffed. Then, he sighed. "When I was attacked last night, the man said my niece had been taken and that if I didn't cooperate and pay up, I'd never see her."

Chase went through each word of that, but there were some huge gaps in the information. Chase tipped his head to Quentin's bandaged shoulder and went to April's side. "Who shot you?" he asked Quentin.

"I don't know. Maybe it was you?" Quentin countered.

That got Quentin a huff from not only just Chase but Jax and April, too. She went closer to the bed and stared down at her brother. "Tell us everything that happened so we can try to prevent any further attacks."

Quentin held the stare for several moments and then eased his head back onto his pillow. "Someone broke into my house yesterday. A man wearing a ski mask. He told me my niece had been kidnapped and that he would take me to her. I didn't believe him. We fought, and I'm pretty sure I managed to cut him with a kitchen knife. I couldn't get to my gun so I ran out the back, and that's when he shot me."

That explained the blood on the floor at his house. However, it didn't mean Quentin was telling the truth. "What happened then?" Chase asked.

"I kept running. I wasn't sure who to trust so I didn't

call the marshals. I haven't trusted them right from the start. So, I made my way here, figuring April would be with you." He paused, glancing at them. Or rather glancing at how close they were standing to each other. "I was right."

Quentin seemed to be implying there was something going on between April and him. Something more than just Bailey.

And he was right.

The old attraction was indeed still there, and anyone within a hundred yards of them could likely see it. Chase wanted to believe he could keep pushing it away, but it just kept coming back. That's why he needed to concentrate on the investigation. Because losing focus now could put Bailey right back in danger.

"Tell me about Renée," Chase insisted.

Quentin blinked as if surprised or just plain uncomfortable by the change in subject. "What does she have to do with this?"

"Maybe everything," April answered. "She was with Bailey when we found her."

More than a blink that time. Quentin's head came off the pillow. "You think she's the one who kidnapped your baby?"

April shook her head. "We're not sure what her role was in all this. Tell me about Renée," she repeated, sounding more like a cop than a sister.

Quentin took a deep breath. "I met her at the bar and we had an affair. A short one because she turned out to be a little too high maintenance for me. I'm talking dozens of calls and texts each day. I know she's in love with me, but I just don't feel the same way about her. I haven't heard from her, though, since I went into WITSEC."

"Does Renée know Crossman?" Chase asked.

If Quentin was faking the surprise from that question, then he was very good at it. "You don't believe she'd team up with Crossman?" He cursed, not waiting for the answer. "Renée knows him, all right. She met Crossman at the bar."

Of course. Crossman spent a lot of time at the bar Quentin owned so it was logical that Renée and he would run into each other. Chase hoped those encounters hadn't led to some unholy alliance.

Chase glanced at Jax, who was already taking out his phone. "I'm on it," Jax said, stepping back into the hall and shutting the door behind him.

"On what?" Quentin demanded. "Who's he calling?"

"The jail," Chase answered. "If Renée visited Crossman, we can maybe get access to their conversations. It's possible Crossman put her up to doing the kidnapping." But then, it was just as possible that Renée was acting on her own. "Was Renée ever pregnant with your child?"

Quentin's eyes widened. "She said she was. Did Renée have a baby?"

"No." But that was the only part of the explanation that Chase managed because the door opened again, and when Jax stuck in his head, Chase knew something was wrong.

"Quentin has a visitor," Jax explained. "The guard's already frisked him. No gun." His attention went to Quentin. Then to April. "The guy says his name is Malcolm Knox and that he's a close friend of yours. He wants to see both Quentin and you now."

APRIL SUCKED IN her breath and held it a moment. And yes, it was indeed Malcolm who came through the door. There wasn't a strand of his sandy-blond hair out of place, and he was wearing one of the pricey black suits that he favored. He was also carrying a huge bouquet of flowers.

"April," Malcolm said. He smiled at her as if this were a social visit.

Chase wasn't smiling, though. "Did you know he was coming here?" he asked her.

She shook her head, glancing back at her brother, but Quentin had a startled expression that was similar to her own. "You know Malcolm?" her brother asked her.

"Yes. And I take it so do you." She folded her arms over her chest and snapped toward Malcolm. "Why are you here?"

Malcolm didn't seem put off by her brusque tone. He went closer to Quentin and placed the flowers on the table next to the bed. "I came to check on you. I was sorry to hear of your injury. Are you all right?"

"I've been better." Quentin was still studying April's reaction. "What's this all about?"

Chase stepped between Malcolm and her. "Start talking. How did you even know Quentin and April were here?"

Malcolm certainly didn't extend a smile to Chase. "You're the marshal. Bailey's biological father." He didn't exactly add any endearment to that label.

"Bailey's *father*," Chase corrected. No endearment for him, either.

Part of April wanted to be flattered that Chase was jealous. After all, Malcolm was good-looking. But that wasn't a jealous look Chase was giving the man. He was a marshal looking at a potential suspect.

The very one Crossman had warned them about.

"Get started on answering those questions I just

asked," Chase demanded. "How did you even know they were here?"

"When I heard there was blood found at Quentin's house, I hired a team of private investigators to start checking the hospitals. I thought if he was seriously hurt, he would need some help."

Chase shook his head. "Quentin wasn't admitted here under his own name."

"I didn't figure he would be," Malcolm readily answered. "Not with April and him being in WITSEC. But I had the PIs check this particular hospital because I thought Quentin might try to come here. Because of your past connection to April."

Past? That was not the right thing to say.

Malcolm wasn't an idiot. At least she didn't think he was. So maybe he was just pushing Chase's buttons on purpose. And in Malcolm's case, April was fairly certain that jealousy was involved here. She hadn't done anything to lead Malcolm on. In fact, she'd been out and out rude to him on numerous occasions, but that hadn't caused him to back off.

"You knew I was in WITSEC?" she asked. "For how long?"

"Practically from the first day I met you." Malcolm paused, smiled again. But this time, there was discomfort in that smile. "I don't allow many people into my life. I've been burned by those who are only after my money. So, after we met at the hospital, I ran a background check on you."

April glared at him. Both Quentin and Chase groaned, but it was Chase who responded. "Nothing would have turned up about April in a normal background check."

"My staff was thorough," Malcolm said as if choosing his words carefully. "And soon they found Quentin."

Quentin didn't just groan that time. He cursed and looked at her. "I had no idea he knew you. He never said." Then, his gaze flew to Malcolm. "What the hell were you trying to do? Get information on April?"

"I was trying to figure out a way to keep Bailey and her safe," Malcolm said without hesitating.

"It wasn't your job to do that," Chase pointed out.

That put some fire in Malcolm's otherwise ice-blue eyes. "Well, you didn't do a very good job of it, did you?"

April had known Malcolm only two months and she'd never seen his temper flare. She was certainly seeing it now. But then, so was Chase's. She didn't want this to turn into a man contest, not when they were so short of answers. Still, Malcolm was giving her the creeps.

"Did you hack into WITSEC files to find me?" she asked, and April didn't bother to make it sound friendly.

Malcolm looked as if she had punched him. "Of course not. I wouldn't have endangered you that way. The PIs used facial recognition software and matched it to some old photos of you they found on the internet."

The marshals had deleted as many photos as they could find, but April had always known there might be some still floating around. That was the main reason the marshals had wanted to place her in a different state, but April had always figured if someone wanted to find her hard enough, they could.

And apparently Malcolm had.

"April," Malcolm said, coming closer to her. At least that's what he tried to do, but Chase blocked his way. Despite that, Malcolm snagged her gaze from over Chase's shoulder. "I know this all must seem strange to you, but what I felt for you was instant. Love at first sight."

She dropped back a step. "You don't even know me."

"That's not true. We spent all that time talking when Bailey was in the intensive care unit. You cried on my shoulder."

Chase glanced back at her.

"I would have cried on anyone's shoulder then," April explained. She huffed, tried to say this in a way that would make it crystal clear to Malcolm. "I don't have those kinds of feelings for you. And I never will."

If he was fazed by that, Malcolm didn't show it. "Forever's a long time. People change. *You* might change."

"Enough of this. Tell me how you know Tony Crossman," Chase came out and demanded.

Malcolm pulled back his shoulders. "I don't know him. Not personally anyway. I've read about what he did, of course, and with Quentin and April scheduled to testify against him at his upcoming trial, I figure that means he'd like to get back at them." He shifted his attention to April. "Is Crossman the one who kidnapped Bailey?"

She lifted her shoulder. "Crossman seems to think you're responsible. Or at least you know something about it."

"I don't!" There it was again. That temper. "I wouldn't hurt you or Bailey. Unlike him." Malcolm jabbed his index finger at Chase.

That put a hard, dangerous look in Chase's eyes. "What the hell do you mean by that?"

However, Malcolm didn't answer. His attention went back to April instead. "There's something you should know. After I found out who you were and that the marshal here was Bailey's father, I had a background check done on him."

"You what?" she snapped.

Chase didn't say a word, but April could practically see every muscle tightening in his body. Despite that, Malcolm still didn't even spare Chase a glance.

"Marshal Crockett didn't tell you?" Malcolm pressed.

April tried to tamp down the uneasiness that was racing through her. She failed. "Tell me what?"

She didn't like that smug look that Malcolm got. Now he looked at Chase, and the smug look intensified tenfold. "The marshal hired a lawyer, and he's planning to challenge you for custody of Bailey."

Chapter Eight

Oh, man. This was not something Chase wanted to discuss with April right now, but judging from how fast her expression went from shock to anger, he didn't have much of a choice.

"You did what?" she asked. Not a shout. No, this was barely a whisper. Probably because her throat had clamped shut.

"Come on. We need to talk," Chase said. It was stating the obvious, but he didn't want April to start an argument with him while they were still in the room with her brother and Malcolm.

Especially Malcolm.

Later, Chase would settle up with that idiot, but for now he had some explaining to do. The question was, would April actually listen? There was only a thin thread of trust between them, and this sure wouldn't help.

She didn't resist but didn't exactly cooperate, either, when Chase took hold of her arm. She slung off his grip but marched out into the hall with him. Since there was a stream of nurses, doctors and visitors, and the guard, too, Chase kept walking until he found a private waiting area.

"Did you hire a lawyer?" April asked the moment he shut the door.

Chase looked her straight in the eyes. "I did. But hear me out before you get more upset."

Too late. April pushed herself away from him and headed to the other side of the room.

"How could you?" She sounded angry. And worse, she sounded hurt.

"I only talked to a lawyer because I thought if I had custody, it would be better for Bailey. She'd have a real home with a large family. A grandmother, aunts, uncles and cousins. I thought she deserved that."

He could also see the anger and hurt evaporating from her body. Well, the anger anyway. And April certainly didn't jump to argue with him about the family part. She just stood there with tears shimmering in her eyes.

"You thought it was best for Bailey, and in a way, it is." April shook her head. "God, Chase. I'd miss her so much. It'd break my heart to lose her."

Cursing himself, cursing Malcolm, too, Chase went to her. "I didn't tell you about visiting the lawyer because I nixed the idea. Yes, Bailey would have a good home at the ranch, but it wouldn't necessarily be a safe one. Crossman's thugs could get to her there."

Of course, they'd gotten to her at the WITSEC house, too, but Chase figured the Crockett ranch was the first place Crossman would send his hired guns to look for her. Then, he could use Bailey to get to April.

April looked up at him. Maybe trying to decide if he was telling her the truth. He was. But after everything that'd gone on between them, Chase wasn't sure she'd believe him. So, he did something to prove it.

Something stupid.

Chase kissed her.

One touch of his mouth on hers and he got a fast reminder of why they'd landed in bed in the first place. This fire. Always there. *Always.* And the fire didn't seem to care that they weren't suited for each other.

After just a few seconds, Chase was ready to force himself away from her and give her permission to slap him into the next county. But when he went to pull away, April took hold of him and held on. She also made that silky sound of pleasure. Just a slight sound that came from deep within her throat, but it was yet another jolting reminder that he was playing with fire.

That didn't stop him.

In fact, it got worse. Because Chase deepened the kiss, dragged her closer until they were plastered against each other. With every part of her touching every part of him. Definitely not good, and thankfully that *not good* part finally made it through to his brain and he stepped back from her.

April stared at him, her breath gusting. "Wow," she muttered. "Was that your way of apologizing?"

"I wish." But unfortunately saying I'm sorry had nothing to do with that kiss.

She nodded as if she knew exactly what he meant. And she probably did. This wasn't a good time for the old attraction to fan these flames. It was a distraction. A nice one that he could still taste and feel. But a distraction nonetheless.

"Does this mean you'll hate me even more now?" she asked.

Chase opened his mouth to answer that and realized he didn't know quite what to say. "I don't hate you," he finally admitted. "I hate what you did." And he also hated he felt things for her he didn't want to feel.

She nodded, might have jumped deeper into this conversation that they shouldn't be having, but the door flew open. Chase automatically pulled his gun, and he didn't holster it when he saw their visitor.

Malcolm.

"I wanted to make sure you were okay," the man said to April.

He volleyed glances between Chase and her, maybe picking up on the vibes still in the room. Or maybe April and he just looked as if they'd kissed each other's brains out. Either way, Malcolm's sour expression said he didn't like it.

"I hope you didn't lie your way out of this," Malcolm snarled when his attention settled on Chase. "You went to see that lawyer and I can prove it."

Chase was about to set things straight with this clown, but April stepped in front of him. "Malcolm, it's time for you to leave."

Obviously, that wasn't the response Malcolm had been expecting. "You're taking his side?"

"Yes. He's Bailey's father. Chase was only thinking about her best interest when he saw the lawyer."

Malcolm threw his hands in the air. "He was trying to take your daughter away from you."

Chase was so tired of this. "*Our* daughter. Mine and April's. And in case you didn't hear her, April just asked you to leave. Now I'm telling you to get out of here."

The anger flared through Malcolm's eyes. "You're using your badge?"

"No. This isn't about a badge. This is about me telling you to leave, or I'll drag you out of here."

That didn't cool down any of Malcolm's anger. "I was there for April and Bailey when you weren't. I gave April comfort when you didn't. And I would have paid any amount of ransom to get Bailey back."

Chase was about to tell this jerk that he hadn't been there to comfort April only because she hadn't thought it was safe to let him know that Bailey had been born. But maybe Malcolm already knew that. Perhaps because Malcolm had been the one who'd planted those cameras and bugs at Chase's house.

Maybe he'd also been the one to kidnap Bailey.

The man's feelings for April seemed obsessive, and if he'd been able to "save" Bailey from the kidnappers, then Malcolm might have believed that would help him win over April.

Malcolm must have realized that his anger wasn't going to earn him any points with April because his expression softened. "Promise me you'll call me if you need anything," he said to her.

"I'll be fine," she answered. Which, of course, wasn't much of an answer in Malcolm's eyes, but the man must have decided that was the best he was going to get right now.

Malcolm nodded, and without giving Chase even another glance, he turned and walked out. Only then did April release the breath she'd been holding.

"I swear, Malcolm wasn't like this when I met him in the hospital," she insisted. "He was nice. Charming, even."

Chase believed her. That was classic stalker behavior, and he was betting if he dug a little deeper into Malcolm's past that he would find a pattern of this kind of behavior.

Well, unless Malcolm was faking it.

"I need to see if there's a connection between Crossman and Malcolm," Chase told her, and he holstered his gun.

She nodded without hesitation, which meant April had already come to the same conclusion. Crossman could have hired or coerced Malcolm into getting close to her so he could have the opportunity to do some very bad things to her.

Like kidnap Bailey.

"You said you didn't meet Malcolm until after Bailey was born," he continued, "but I saw that lawyer three months ago. So, how did Malcolm know that?"

He could almost see the thoughts racing through her head. "You're thinking Malcolm had me, and you, in his sights before he introduced himself to me."

Chase shrugged. "Either that or his PIs got very lucky. I only visited that lawyer once, and I didn't exactly share the news with anyone. In fact, I didn't even tell anyone in my family."

April closed her eyes a moment, shuddered. "If Malcolm's working for Crossman, then he could have found me right after I went into WITSEC. Maybe Crossman didn't want to kill a pregnant woman so he waited until after Bailey was born."

Maybe but that didn't explain why Malcolm or another of Crossman's hired guns hadn't killed April afterward. Unless Malcolm had developed feelings for her.

Not exactly a settling thought.

He really needed to find out if there was a connection between Malcolm and Crossman.

Chase heard the footsteps in the hall, and he reached for his gun again. False alarm this time because it was Jax.

"You're not going to believe who just called the hospital," Jax said. "Renée. And she's demanding to speak to Quentin. I've got her on hold for now, but I thought you might want to listen in on the conversation."

He did. "Did Renée say where she was?" Chase asked.

"Not yet. I'm hoping she'll let something slip." Jax sounded as if he had a score to settle with the woman. And in a way, he did. Because Jax could have been hurt or worse when Renée escaped. Plus, innocent people didn't usually try to run from the law. The trouble was, Chase wasn't exactly sure how Renée fit into this mess, but maybe he'd find out.

"I figure Renée might say more if she thinks she's just talking to Quentin," Jax explained. "But if the conversation doesn't go our direction, I'll let her know we're there."

Good plan. They hurried back to Quentin's room. Quentin was sitting up in his bed, the hospital phone already in his hand. Jax pressed the button to take the call off hold and then put it on speaker.

"Renée?" Quentin said.

"Thank God. It's so good to hear your voice." Renée's words rushed out with her breath. "How badly are you hurt?"

"I'll live. Where are you?" Quentin asked. A question that Jax had probably told him to ask.

"I'd rather not say over the phone, just in case someone's listening. But I need to see you. I've missed you so much, Quentin, and there are things I have to tell you."

"What things?" Quentin pressed.

"Can't get into that now. But later. How soon can we meet?"

Quentin looked at Jax, and Jax jotted something down on the notepad next to the phone. "Soon," Quentin read from the note. "Can you come here to the hospital? I'd love to see you."

Renée hesitated. "I doubt that would be safe. I mean, they're probably guarding your room, right?"

Quentin relayed the next part of what Jax wrote. "I can get rid of the guard. Just come here so we can talk."

More hesitation. "Promise me this isn't some kind of trap," Renée finally said.

The door opened, and a nurse pushing a wheelchair started to come in, but Jax motioned for her to wait.

"I swear it's not a trap," Quentin said to Renée before Jax could write down his next response. "I need to see you, but I also need to find out some other things. Like why my WITSEC identity was blown. April's, too. Any idea who's responsible for that?"

"I don't know," Renée answered right away. "I'm still working on that."

"Is that why you were with the men who kidnapped my niece?"

Renée let that question hang in the air for several moments. "We can talk about that when I see you. Quentin, I've been through so much." A hoarse sob tore from her mouth. "I have to tell you about the baby."

"Did you really have a baby?" Quentin snapped. "You told me you were pregnant, but I wasn't sure if it was a false alarm or not."

More hesitation. "We can talk about it when I see you. I can be there in an hour. Is that enough time for you to get rid of the guard?"

Quentin waited until Jax nodded. "That's enough time. Don't be late."

"I won't be. I love you, Quentin."

He didn't respond, and after several moments, Renée

ended the call. "I take it I won't be meeting her alone," Quentin immediately said to Jax.

"You won't be meeting her at all. In fact, she won't even make it into the hospital. I'll arrest her in the parking lot." Jax went to the door, opened it, and the nurse was still there.

"I have to take Mr. Taylor to have an MRI on his shoulder," she said. Taylor was the alias Quentin had used when he'd been admitted to the hospital.

"Hold on a sec," Chase insisted.

He checked her name tag. Kitty Gagnon, and the woman made a sound of surprise when he took her picture with his phone. Then, Chase made a call to confirm she was indeed a nurse. It took him several minutes to work his way through to the hospital chief, but he verified that the woman was indeed Kitty Gagnon and that she was a nurse assigned to this particular floor. Only then did Chase motion for her to get Quentin into the wheelchair.

However, before the nurse could take him out of the room, April caught Quentin's hand. "Did you have anything, and I mean *anything*, to do with what's been happening?"

Quentin cursed, shook his head, but it took him a long time to say the answer aloud. "No."

April let go of him, and the nurse wheeled him away with the guard following along behind them.

"Go ahead and get April out of here," Jax told Chase, and he took out his phone. No doubt to start getting backup in place so he could arrest Renée when she arrived. "I'll follow you out."

Chase didn't waste any time getting her out of the room and heading toward the exit. "You believe Quentin when he said he didn't have any part in this?" Chase asked her.

She huffed, pushed her hair from her face. "I wish I did. It'd help us narrow down our suspects."

Yes. Because three was too many. Or there were possibly even four if Renée, Malcolm or Quentin weren't working for Crossman.

What Chase needed to do was make a trip to the jail. Not to talk with Crossman. He wasn't sure the man would tell the truth. But maybe the visitors' logs and the guards would be able to give him some information that would link one of their suspects to Crossman. If he could just make that connection, then other charges could be filed against Crossman and his assets could be frozen.

Chase went ahead of her when they reached the door, but he'd barely made it a step outside when he saw something he didn't want to see.

Renée.

The woman was standing next to a black SUV, and she had binoculars pressed to her eyes.

"Get back inside," Chase told April.

It was already too late. The shot slammed through the air. And it hadn't come from outside.

It had come from behind them.

The shooter was in the hospital.

Chapter Nine

Before April even realized what was happening, Chase pulled her to the floor and to the side of a chair. Not a second too soon. Because another shot came their way and blasted into the glass surrounding the sliding doors.

Oh, God. Someone was trying to kill them again.

Bailey wasn't with them this time, but there were plenty of people in the hospital who could be hurt.

There were screams and shouts, people running and trying to get out of the path of those shots. The gunman didn't seem focused on any of them, though. The shots were coming in the direction of Chase, Jax and her.

"You see the shooter?" Jax asked. He, too, had dropped to the floor and was to the side of a display case. Not much cover at all.

Chase shook his head. "But I did see Renée in the parking lot."

April's heart was already pounding, and that only made it worse. She doubted this was a coincidence, especially since the woman had said it'd be an hour before she arrived for her meeting with Quentin. Maybe Renée knew that would spur Chase and her to leave so that Renée could have someone gun them down.

But the shots weren't outside. They were coming from the very hall that led to Quentin's room.

April wanted to believe a hired gun couldn't have gotten inside, but there was no metal detector in the small hospital, and the security guard was with Quentin.

"Keep an eye on the parking lot," Chase told her. "If you see Renée or anyone else coming closer, let me know."

She would. But she also doubted Renée would just come walking into the middle of this. Well, unless Renée planned on taking some shots at them, too.

While keeping his body in front of hers, Chase called for backup. Since the sheriff's office was just up the street, it wouldn't take Jericho and the other deputies long to get there. But it still might not be in time to stop someone from getting hurt.

Heavens, was this shooter after her? Or was this some kind of ploy to get to Quentin?

April didn't have time to think about that, though. There was another shot, followed by a woman's scream. "Help me," she shouted.

Chase glanced around the chair and cursed. So did Jax. Judging from the woman's frantic pleas, April figured the gunman had taken a hostage.

"Tell Jericho to approach through the back of the hospital," Chase whispered to Jax, and he leaned out.

A shot came right at him, and he ducked back behind cover.

"Let her go," Chase called out. "She has no part in this."

"She does if she'll get me out of here," the gunman shouted back.

April peered around the edge of the chair and spotted them. Like the other men who'd kidnapped Bailey, the gunman was wearing a ski mask, and he was using his hostage as a human shield. The woman was a nurse and couldn't have been more than twenty-five. And she looked terrified, her eyes pleading for someone to do something to save her.

"What do you want?" Chase asked the man. "Who sent you here?"

"I could answer that, but it'd get me killed in a really bad way. No thanks. So, here's how this is going to work. You're going to let me walk out of here, and once I'm sure I'm out of the line of fire, I'll let her go."

April replayed his words and shook her head. "Why would he come here without a plan to get out? A plan that didn't involve taking a random hostage? It's too risky. He could have just waited outside and gunned us down."

Chase agreed so quickly that it made her realize he'd already come to that same conclusion. And that meant maybe the gunman wasn't there to kill them but to create a diversion.

"Quentin," she said.

"Stay down," Chase warned her.

April had no intentions of running out there since she'd only be shot, but she prayed the security guard would be able to protect her brother if this attack was indeed aimed at him.

"Help me," the nurse begged again, and judging from the sound of her voice, her captor was moving her deeper into the hall. Where he would no doubt try to escape with her.

Unfortunately, there were too many ways for him to do just that.

There were clinics on one side of the hall, and most

of them had exits to the parking lot. If the thug made it that far, he could get away. That wouldn't be good for the nurse. Or for them. Because he wouldn't be able to give them answers as to why this was happening, and he might kill the nurse instead of letting her go.

"You have a clean shot?" Chase asked Jax.

Jax shook his head and checked his phone when it dinged. "Jericho's just now pulling into the parking lot. He spotted Renée, and she's armed."

No. That meant it might not be safe for Jericho to get out of his cruiser. Of course, that probably wouldn't stop him, but Renée could certainly slow him down if she started shooting.

The nurse screamed, and when April glanced at her, she saw something she definitely didn't want to see. The nurse was fighting to get loose, and her captor was fighting back. He bashed her against the head with his gun and then took aim at her. Ready to kill her.

Chase reacted fast. So fast that it was over before April even saw it coming. He leaned out from the chair and fired two shots, the sounds blasting through the hospital.

April held her breath, adding another prayer for the nurse. But it wasn't the nurse who'd been shot. It was the gunman. He crumpled into a heap on the floor.

"I need to get April away from this door," Chase told Jax. Probably because of Renée. The woman could come running in at any moment. "Stay behind me," Chase added to her.

April got to her feet, trailing along behind him as Chase made his way to the guy he'd just shot. The nurse was still screaming, but several of her coworkers rushed forward to pull her away.

When Chase made it to the man, he leaned down, retrieved his gun and stripped off the ski mask. April got just a glimpse of his face.

A stranger.

She supposed that was better than it being someone she knew, but this was the third armed thug who'd attacked them, and it made her wonder just how many assassins had been hired to come after them.

Or to come after her brother.

"Watch our backs," Chase called out to Jax.

Chase was watching all around them, too, as he made his way down the hall. No sign of the guard outside her brother's room, but then the man had gone with Quentin and the nurse to have the MRI done.

There were two nurses who were still cowering behind their station, and it probably didn't help their panic when they saw Chase's gun.

"Where's the patient who was in this room?" Chase asked them.

"Still in radiology," one of them answered and reached for the phone. "I'll call over there."

It seemed to take an eternity for her to do that. And while April waited, she tried to tamp down her fear. Hard to do that, though, with the adrenaline still pumping through her.

She couldn't hear the nurse's whispered conversation with whomever the woman had called, but April had no trouble figuring out that something was wrong. The nurse was trembling even harder when she finished the call.

"I called the receptionist at the check-in desk in radiology and she said no one's answering in the MRI room," the nurse finally said. "But that's where they took the patient and it's just at the end of the hall on the right."

That caused April's fear and adrenaline to soar, but she tried not to think the worst. Maybe the nurse and her brother had taken cover when they heard the shots.

Chase got them moving again. Kept looking around as well, and they made their way farther down the hall. When they reached the door for radiology, Chase eased it open.

And then he cursed.

April's heart went to her knees. Her brother wasn't there. The room was empty, but there were definite signs of a struggle. Equipment and a wheelchair had been toppled over.

"They took them," someone said.

With his gun ready, Chase pivoted in the direction of the voice. It was the nurse, Kitty Gagnon, and she was crying and hiding behind an examination curtain.

"They took the patient, Mr. Taylor," Kitty added.

"Who took them?" Chase snapped.

But she only shook her head. "Two armed men." A hoarse sob tore from her throat. "God, I think they killed him."

CHASE LOOKED OVER his notes from the phone calls he'd just made. Notes that he'd need to file an official report, but he didn't like much of what he'd jotted down. Quentin was missing.

Maybe dead.

And Renée was nowhere to be found. She'd managed to escape during all the gunfire.

He figured it wasn't a coincidence that Renée and those gunmen had been at the hospital at the same time. In fact he hoped it wasn't a coincidence. Because if Renée and her hired guns had kidnapped Quentin, then it likely meant the man was still alive. Renée hadn't seemed interested in killing Quentin, only renewing a romantic relationship with him. Of course, if Quentin wasn't willing to pretend he would do that, Renée might kill him anyway.

Chase made his way from the deputy's desk he'd been using and went to Jericho's office. April was there, right where he'd left her nearly an hour earlier. However, her expression had changed considerably. She no longer looked shell-shocked and ready to fall apart. She was smiling. And it took Chase a moment to realize she was smiling at something on the computer screen.

Bailey.

"Levi set up the computer so we'd be able to see Bailey at the safe house," April explained, turning the screen so Chase could see. "He said it was okay to do this, that no one could hack into the feed."

"Levi's right," Chase assured her, and it didn't take long before he, too, was smiling. Bailey was in her carry seat and she was grabbing her toes while making babbling sounds.

"I was just telling April that the baby's doing great," Levi said. "Big appetite, lots of diapers."

"Are you sure you know how to change a diaper?" Chase asked. It was a valid question since Levi was the only one of his siblings who didn't have a child.

"You're kidding, right? I got plenty of practice with Matthew," Levi reminded him.

Jax's son. Yeah, they'd all gotten plenty of practice with him since Jax was a widower, and they'd all pitched in to help from time to time.

"Gotta say, though," Levi went on, "I'm glad to have

a niece even if she is outnumbered by her nephews. I'll bet Mom can't wait to get her hands on her only granddaughter."

Levi no doubt hadn't meant that to be anything other than lighthearted, but it caused April's smile to fade some. Probably because it was a reminder that there might not be any opportunities for Bailey to get to know her grandmother or the rest of the family. Of course, April's look could also have something to do with that visit Chase had made to the lawyer.

Or that kiss.

There'd been nothing to smile about in that particular department. It'd broken down walls between them that were best left standing. Chase didn't consider himself an emotional sort, but he wasn't sure he could handle another heart-stomping from April. Especially since he needed to be doing whatever it took to keep things amicable between them.

Bailey started fussing, and as if he were an old pro at tending babies, Levi scooped her up in his arms. "It's bottle time. I'll call you back after her nap." He paused. "Not that I mind babysitting duty, but when do you think you'll make it back here?"

"Soon," Chase answered.

That was wishful thinking on his part. More than anything, Chase wanted to be back at that safe house, giving his daughter a bottle and watching her for real, not via a computer screen.

But there was a huge problem.

Those two gunmen who'd taken Quentin. Chase couldn't be sure they weren't lurking around, prepared to attack the moment he stepped outside with April. Of course, eventually they'd have to leave the sheriff's office, but he was hoping those gunmen would be found, and jailed, before that happened.

Levi cut the video feed, the screen going blank, and the rest of April's smile went blank with it. Something Chase totally understood.

"I miss her, too," he said.

April nodded, blinked back tears that filled her eyes. "It's hard to believe how much you can love someone so much."

Yes, he got that, too. "It feels as if she's been in my life forever." But he figured most parents felt the same.

That didn't seem to do anything to put April in a better mood. "I don't suppose the nurse was able to describe the men who took Quentin?"

"Only that they were wearing ski masks. She said the two men stormed into radiology, grabbed Quentin and dragged him out the back exit of the hospital. She heard two shots fired."

April drew in a long breath. "The nurse didn't actually see, though, if Quentin was shot?"

"No. But there's more." And now here was the part Chase really didn't want to have to explain. However, he couldn't keep it from her. "Jericho interviewed an eyewitness in that back parking lot, and he said he saw one of the men fire shots into the air."

"Into the air?" April stayed quiet a moment, obviously giving that some thought. "You believe Quentin faked his own kidnapping?"

"I believe it's possible. Maybe he didn't want to have to answer any more questions about how he'd gotten injured." He paused again. "I found out through one of the CIs that your brother did indeed owe money to the wrong person. A loan shark. Word on the street is that he's the one who attacked Quentin and that it could get a whole lot worse for your brother if he doesn't pay back the money."

"And Quentin could have wanted to use the ransom money to do that," April finished for him. "Or he could have just been trying to escape before the loan shark got to him again."

Chase had come to the same conclusion. Too bad they couldn't find Quentin so they could ask him. Of course, that didn't mean he'd tell them what had actually happened. Honesty wasn't Quentin's strong suit.

April looked up at him. "Is it true—will we be going back to the safe house soon like you told Levi?"

"Hopefully. I'm just waiting on a call from Jericho." And hoping his brother had found those gunmen.

She nodded, probably reading between the lines on that. "Anything new on Renée?"

He had to shake his head. "The dead gunman is a wash for now, too. No ID, and his prints aren't in the system." And with Rooks still not talking, Chase was still way short on answers.

"Are you okay?" he asked her.

April's gaze met his, and he was pretty sure she knew he wasn't just asking about her in the general sense. "You mean that kiss."

Bingo. She zoomed right in on that.

"I thought you'd want to see it as a lapse in judgment," she said. "And nothing more."

That was indeed how he wanted to see it, all right. But parts of him were struggling to keep that view. "How did you see it?" he asked, despite the fact that it was stupid to continue this conversation on any level.

She stood, meeting him eye-to-eye. "You really want to know?" But she didn't wait for an answer. "I see it as a reminder of how things led to us getting Bailey. A reminder that's still there. Don't worry," April quickly added. "I know it's not what you want so it won't happen again."

Heck. For some reason that riled him. So much so that Chase took hold of her and kissed her again.

It wasn't the powerhouse kiss they'd had in the hospital. Just a quick brush of his mouth to hers to remind her that if they didn't put some distance between them, that it would indeed happen again. And it might have happened a lot sooner.

Like instantly.

If Chase hadn't heard someone come into the sheriff's office.

"Wait here," he told April, and he stepped into the hallway to see Jax ushering a dark-haired man through the metal detectors.

Chase didn't recognize the guy, but he was tall, thin. Late thirties. And while he was wearing jeans and a T-shirt, Chase was betting that both had designer labels on them.

"Marshal Crockett," the man said, his attention going straight to Chase. "I'm Shane Hackett, Renée's husband. I believe I know where you can find her."

Chapter Ten

April went into the hall when she heard their visitor. *Finally.* This could be the break they were looking for.

"Where's Renée?" April asked while hurrying into the squad room. Something that Chase obviously didn't want her to do. But if they could find Renée, they might be able to learn if she or someone else was behind the attack.

"You're Quentin's sister." Shane studied her for a moment, disapproval written all over his face. Disapproval maybe just for Quentin or perhaps because she happened to be the sister of the man who'd had an affair with his wife.

Shane slipped his hand in his jeans pocket, a move that sent both Jax and Chase reaching for their guns. Even though Shane had obviously cleared the metal detector, that didn't mean he still couldn't be dangerous. But it wasn't a weapon that he pulled out. It was a piece of paper, and he handed it to Chase.

"Those are the addresses of mine and Renée's properties. Some aren't in our names. My real estate company owns them. The first one is a cabin only about thirty miles from here. That's my best guess as to where she'd go, but the others are possibilities, too."

"I'm on it," Jax said. He took the paper and headed for

the phone. No doubt so he could get someone out there to check the place since it wasn't in the jurisdiction of the Appaloosa Pass Sheriff's Department.

"If you believe she could be there," April said, "why didn't you go out and check?"

Clearly, Shane wasn't comfortable with that, and he took his time answering. "Because Renée made it clear that she didn't want to see me. She said if I tried to find her, that she'd harm herself. I figured you'd do a better job protecting and restraining her than I could."

April thought about that a moment. It was possibly true. From everything they'd learned about Shane, he did still care for his wife. Though April had no idea why.

"Has Renée been in contact with you recently?" Chase asked the man.

Shane nodded without hesitation. "She called me yesterday, said she might have gotten into something over her head and wanted me to give her as much cash as I had on hand, that she'd have a courier pick up the money. She didn't want to take anything from her accounts because she said someone was after her."

Chase tapped his badge. "Someone is. She's a suspect in the kidnapping of a baby and two attacks."

Shane hadn't shown much emotion. Until hearing that. He didn't stagger back exactly, but he suddenly looked very unsteady on his feet. "Renée's off her meds. That's not good. Because she does impulsive things without her meds."

"Does that mean you believe she's responsible for the kidnapping?" Chase asked.

Now Shane paused, groaned and scrubbed his hand over his face. "Possibly." He looked at April again. "Does this have anything to do with your brother?"

"I honestly don't know but maybe. Renée was at the hospital earlier when my brother was kidnapped." Or when he faked a kidnapping, that is. April had no idea which—not yet.

Shane's jaw tightened. "Renée was with Quentin." Now there was another emotion, one that April had no trouble figuring out. Jealousy.

"I don't know if they were together or just happened to be there at the same time. As I said, my brother's missing, too."

Shane's next groan was louder. "He's bad news for her, you know."

Yes, April did know that. But she thought the relationship might have been toxic for both of them. "Was Renée ever pregnant?"

Shane's nod was slow in coming. "She was, but she miscarried about five months ago."

Only about a month after Quentin had gone into WIT-SEC. As emotionally invested as Renée was in Quentin, April wondered if that had triggered the miscarriage.

April stared at Shane. "Was it my brother's baby?"

"Renée said he was the father," Shane admitted almost hesitantly.

"Was he?" April pressed.

"Yes," Shane answered after another long pause. "Renée can be unstable when she's off her meds, but she didn't lie about being in love with your brother. After Quentin went into WITSEC and she lost the baby, she tried to kill herself."

That didn't sound so much like love, but April knew her brother didn't always bring out the best in people.

"Look, I just want you to find her," Shane continued,

FREE Merchandise is 'in the Cards' for you!

Dear Reader,

We're giving away FREE MERCHANDISE!

Seriously, we'd like to reward you for reading this novel by giving you **FREE MERCHANDISE** worth over **$20** retail. And no purchase is necessary!

You see the Jack of Hearts sticker above? Paste that sticker in the box on the Free Merchandise Voucher inside. Return the Voucher promptly...and we'll send you valuable Free Merchandise!

Thanks again for reading one of our novels—and enjoy your Free Merchandise with our compliments!

Pam Powers

Pam Powers

P.S. Look inside to see what Free Merchandise is **"in the cards"** for you!

W

e'd like to send you two free books like the one you are enjoying now. Your two books have a combined price of over $10 retail, but they are yours to keep absolutely FREE! We'll even send you 2 wonderful surprise gifts. You can't lose!

REMEMBER: Your Free Merchandise, consisting of **2 Free Books** and **2 Free Gifts**, is worth over $20 retail! No purchase is necessary, so please send for your Free Merchandise today.

Get TWO FREE GIFTS!

We'll also send you 2 wonderful FREE GIFTS (worth about $10 retail), in addition to your 2 Free books!

Visit us at:

www.ReaderService.com

▲ If offer card is missing write to: Reader Service, P.O. Box 1867, Buffalo, NY 14240-1867 or visit www.ReaderService.com ▲

BUSINESS REPLY MAIL
FIRST-CLASS MAIL   PERMIT NO. 717   BUFFALO, NY

POSTAGE WILL BE PAID BY ADDRESSEE

READER SERVICE
PO BOX 1867
BUFFALO NY 14240-9952

NO POSTAGE
NECESSARY
IF MAILED
IN THE
UNITED STATES

"so she can get the help she needs. Just promise me you won't hurt her if you find her."

"I can't make a promise like that," Chase snapped. "But I can tell you if she's behind the kidnappings and the attacks, I will find her and I'll arrest her. Because there was a woman killed by one of those thugs. If Renée hired them, then she'll be charged with murder."

Of course, Shane must have known that, but it clearly bothered him to hear it spelled out. He reached in his pocket, took out a business card that he handed to Chase. "If you arrest her, call me so I can get her a lawyer. Am I free to go?"

"Not just yet. I need to ask you a few more questions." Chase looked back at Jax. "Why don't you go ahead and take April to Jericho's office?"

April was about to protest, but then Chase tipped his head to the windows. The blinds were all down, and the glass was reinforced and bullet resistant, but it was still risky for her to be out there. Risky for Chase, too, but April doubted she'd be able to get him to leave until he was certain he'd gotten everything he could from Shane.

Jax ushered her to Jericho's office, but he didn't leave once she was there. In fact, he checked the window to make sure it was secure. It was. And he positioned himself in the doorway. Guarding her and keeping watch over Chase.

"You think Shane could have brought hired guns with him?" she asked.

"No." And that's all Jax said for several moments. "I don't think Shane had anything to do with the stuff that happened. But if Renée wants to silence him so he can't help us find her, she might have her goons try to kill him."

April hadn't even considered that. Heck, she wasn't even positive the woman was an actual threat to anyone but herself, but Jax obviously felt she was capable of murder. And maybe she was.

Jax continued to look around the squad room. Continued to glance back at her, as well.

"Sorry you drew the short straw on guarding me," April said after one of Jax's glances looked more like a glare. "I know I'm not someone you actually want to protect."

No glare. But he did frown and seemed a little puzzled. "I don't hold a grudge against you."

"You should. I made a mistake."

"And it seems as if you've paid for it a couple times over," Jax countered.

Now she was the one who frowned. "You don't have to be nice to me."

"I know. But I don't want to stand in the way of Chase getting to raise his baby even if it means he's got to move and that we might not be able to see him for a long time. If ever. Plus, I also figure he's got feelings for you. After all, he slept with you, and Chase isn't the one-night stand sort."

No, he wasn't, but it hadn't been feelings that had caused him to take her to his bed. Well, not love-related kinds of feelings anyway.

"I think Chase started out just wanting to lend me a shoulder. I was upset." An understatement. And the shoulder he'd lent had turned to a heavy kissing session. Then more.

"You have feelings for him, too," Jax tossed out there. "Are you in love with him?"

April nearly choked on the quick breath she sucked

in. "No." She was almost certain of that. Almost. "What I feel for him is complicated."

"Yeah," Jax agreed.

She heard the voice of experience. No doubt because his relationship with his late wife, Paige, had fallen into that same *complicated* category. Despite having a young child, they'd divorced, only for Paige to be murdered by the Moonlight Strangler.

April heard the footsteps, and Jax stepped back from the doorway to let Chase into the room. "I didn't get anything more from Shane," he said. "But I believe he's genuinely worried about Renée."

So did April. Chase opened his mouth to add something else, but his phone rang before he could say anything.

He glanced at the screen, cursed. "What now?"

April hurried to his side to see Unknown Caller on the phone. Her heart sank. This couldn't be good. Chase hit the answer button and put it on speaker.

"Marshal Crockett," the caller said. Not a normal voice, either. The person was speaking through a scrambler, which made it impossible to know if this was any of their suspects. "We need to speak about Quentin Landis. And by *we*, I mean me, you and his sister, April."

Even though she was just a few inches from Chase, she moved even closer to him. "What about my brother?" she asked.

"Do you want to see him alive again?" But the caller continued without waiting for her to respond. "Then, you'll pay up. The ransom is a quarter of a million in cash. I'm giving you two hours to get the money."

She'd known right from the start that a ransom demand might come, but it knotted her stomach to hear it. "That's not enough time," April argued. "I'd need at least a day."

Chase motioned for her to stay quiet. "How do we even know for sure you have Quentin?" he pressed. "You could have heard about the kidnapping and be someone just trying to capitalize on it."

Sweet heaven. April hadn't even considered that. She'd gotten so caught up in her emotional reaction that she hadn't realized this could all be a hoax.

Maybe even one put together by Quentin himself.

"I want to speak to Quentin," Chase went on when the caller didn't say anything. "I want proof that he's actually with you and that he's still alive."

More silence. April heard some shuffling around, some whispers, and for a moment she thought the kidnapper was going to refuse. But finally she heard her brother's voice.

"April, I'm so sorry," Quentin said. "I didn't want to involve you in this."

More shuffling sounds. "There, you heard him," the kidnapper said. "Now get that money together. I'm not giving you a day, either. I want the cash within twelve hours. I'll call you back with the drop-off point." And with that, the kidnapper ended the call.

"You're sure that was Quentin?" Jax asked her.

April nodded. "But I'm not sure if this is a hoax or not. If Crossman had him kidnapped, he probably would have just killed Quentin. And I doubt Renée would be asking for a ransom."

"Shane said she asked him for cash," Jax pointed out.

"True. She might have done that just so she could pay off the hired gun who rescued her when you were bringing her into the sheriff's office," Chase answered. "Or she could want money so she could hide out for a while."

That made sense. "The loan shark could have kidnapped Quentin, though." April gave a heavy sigh. Because it might be true. And even if it wasn't, if Quentin had put all of this together, not getting the cash was still too big of a risk to take.

April reached for the phone. "I'll call the bank and start the process to get the money."

But Chase stopped her. "Think this through. This could be Crossman's work after all. He could be planning on having you make the ransom drop so he can kill both Quentin and you."

That caused her heart to skip a beat. Because it was exactly the sort of plan that Crossman would put together.

"That means if the kidnapper demands you do the drop, you have to refuse," Chase added.

And that kind of refusal could get Quentin killed.

April hated that her brother had gotten himself into hot water with the loan shark. It was possible this was all of his own making. Of course, it was just as possible that he was innocent. Of the kidnapping anyway.

"I won't do the ransom drop," she assured Chase. "I hope you won't, either."

He shrugged. "It'd be the best way to figure out who's really behind this."

But it would also put him right smack in the middle of danger. Of course, that was true of anyone who made that drop.

While April phoned the bank, both Chase and Jax stepped away to make their own calls. It took April several minutes to work her way through to the bank manager and to give him the security information that would allow him to access her savings and trust fund. Even though she was certain the manager was suspicious that she was withdrawing such a large amount, he didn't question it when she asked for it to be delivered to the sheriff's office.

By the time she was done, Jax had already finished his call, but Chase was still on the phone.

"The money will be here in about six hours," she relayed to Jax.

He nodded. "The sheriff over in Raymond Creek checked that cabin Shane told us about. Renée wasn't there, and there was no sign that anyone had been there in a while."

Too bad. In a best-case scenario, Renée would have been there with Quentin so that Renée could be arrested and April could have a long chat with her brother.

"Still no word back on the other addresses," Jax continued. "We might get lucky with one of them, though."

They certainly needed a huge dose of luck, but after glancing at Chase's expression, she doubted that's what they were going to get. "What's wrong?" she came out and asked.

"I had the Rangers do a thorough background check on Malcolm and there's a red flag. A couple of them, actually. Malcolm was a close friend of Tina Murdock."

That put her heart right in her throat. April shook her head. "Malcolm never said anything about knowing the cop who was killed." The cop whose blood was on her hands.

"I didn't think so. I also doubt Malcolm met you by accident at the hospital when Bailey was born. According to one of Malcolm's business associates, he was torn up when Tina was murdered."

The thoughts started to race through h
up enough to want to get revenge on my broth

"Possibly," Chase admitted.

April tried to go back through all the conversa
she'd ever had with Malcolm, including the most recent
one in the hospital. He'd said nothing to indicate he was
out to do her harm, but that didn't mean that wasn't exactly what he had in mind.

"Are you thinking Malcolm could have kidnapped
Quentin?" Jax asked.

Chase cursed. "He could have, but there's more. I finally got the list of Crossman's visitors, and in the last
three months, Malcolm has visited him four times."

April certainly hadn't seen that coming. Great day.
"Why would Malcolm visit the man responsible for his
friend's murder?"

"I'm not sure. The guards recorded all of Crossman's
visitors, but those particular conversations have a lot of
static, making it impossible to hear what they're saying."

April doubted that was a coincidence. "How could
that have happened?" she asked Chase.

"Malcolm probably sneaked in some kind of jamming
device."

Of course. But that didn't answer the big questions.
"Why would Malcolm do that? What did he say to Crossman that he didn't want anyone else to know?"

Chase checked the time. "I'm not sure, but you can
wait here with Jax while I find out. I'm going to the
prison right now to have a chat with Crossman."

Chapter Eleven

Chase wasn't even sure this was worth the risk—visiting Crossman in jail. And he especially wasn't sure it was worth the risk to bring April with him. However, April had made a pretty convincing argument—that since she was Crossman's target, she wanted to be the one to confront him about the kidnapping and attacks.

And about those visits from Malcolm.

Chase wanted to confront the man, too, and considering that Crossman was a piece of slime, he just might spill everything about Malcolm. Well, if there was anything to spill, but it wasn't looking good for the man since Malcolm had a connection to both Crossman and a dead cop.

"I hope Bailey will be okay," April said while they waited for the guards to bring in Crossman. "Other than the kidnapping, this is the longest I've ever been away from her. When she was in the hospital, I slept there."

That didn't surprise him. But it did rile Chase a little that he hadn't had the opportunity to do the same thing. "Bailey will be fine, and once we're done here we can go back to the safe house." Where he hoped April would stay put until he had gotten their new WITSEC identities.

Of course, Chase was hoping that would be soon. Or at least part of him was hoping that. But the thought of turning in his badge for good made it feel as if someone was squeezing the life right out of him.

April fidgeted in the chair, glanced around, checked the time. "Nervous?" he asked.

"Impatient and ready for answers. I never got a sense that Malcolm hated me and wanted revenge."

"People don't always show you what's really going on in their heads," Chase reminded her.

She stared at him, as if looking for some deeper meaning in that remark. And there was one. It was aimed at Quentin, though April seemed to have gotten the big picture on her scummy brother.

"Are we talking about the kisses now?" she asked.

All right, so her train of thought hadn't exactly gone in the same direction as his. Not that his thoughts ever strayed too far from those kisses. Or from her.

"No," he answered.

April continued to stare at him, the corner of her mouth lifting. Almost a smile. Despite the cruddy situation they were in, it was nice to see she could manage even a half smile.

"It's always like this between us," she said. "I'm a criminal. A former one anyway. And you're a lawman. Not exactly a match made in heaven."

She was right. That kind of fire had a completely different origin than heaven.

"Maybe it was an opposites-attract thing," he suggested.

The slight smile returned for a moment, vanished, and it seemed as if she had something to say to him, that maybe it'd been a whole lot more than just opposites attracting. However, she didn't get a chance because at that very moment the guard ushered Crossman into the visiting area.

Despite having been in jail for the past six months, Crossman hadn't changed that much. Heavily muscled, bald and a nose that'd been broken a time or two. He looked exactly like the thug that he was.

Crossman's smile certainly wasn't a slight one. He flashed them a big grin when his gaze met Chase's. Then April's. The grin stayed in place as Crossman sat in the chair on the other side of the Plexiglas partition and picked up the phone.

Chase picked up the phone on his side, too, and he held it so that both April and he would be able to hear the conversation. Of course, that meant more close contact between them.

"April," Crossman greeted. "You're looking a little frazzled, like you haven't had much sleep. Something bothering you?"

"Yes," she readily admitted. "Tell me about your visits with Malcolm Knox."

For just a second, there was a flash of surprise in Crossman's mud-brown eyes. "They were just chitchat."

"That's a lie," Chase snapped. "You warned us about him. Why?"

The slight smile returned, and Crossman leaned back as far in the chair as he could. Which wasn't very far considering he was cuffed and wearing leg chains.

"Malcolm is somewhat of a mystery," Crossman finally said. "And I wasn't sure if he wanted to kill you for your part in that cop's death. They were good friends, you know."

Because April's arm was touching his, Chase felt her

tense. "Did Malcolm say anything about getting back at me for that?" she asked.

"Not specifically, but I got the feeling he wanted to do you and Quentin some harm. Especially Quentin."

"You also want to do us harm so we can't testify against you," April pointed out. "So, why warn us about Malcolm? Or were you afraid Malcolm would do the job you wanted your own thugs to do?"

"Interesting theory. But you're wrong. I don't want you or Quentin dead. Punished, yes, for turning traitor on me. Dead, no. I've known where you were for weeks. *Months*," Crossman corrected.

Chase tried not to look shocked and reminded himself that anything that came out of Crossman's mouth was probably a lie.

"If you found them that long ago, why didn't you do anything about it?" Chase asked.

"I didn't say I knew where Quentin was. Only April. Quentin has a strange habit of not being where he's supposed to be."

Chase shrugged. "Then why not just go after April?"

"Because as I said, I didn't want either Quentin or her dead. I wanted them to lead me to my former CPA. Jasmine Bronson. I need to…talk to her. Because you see, when my trial eventually starts, I'll need Jasmine to tell the truth, that it wasn't me she saw shooting that cop, that she was mistaken. In fact, I'd like for Jasmine to remember that it was either Quentin or someone else who pulled that trigger."

That was a not so subtle way of saying that Crossman wanted to intimidate the CPA into lying. And the problem was, Crossman might be able to do just that if he could find her. Apparently, he hadn't, yet.

According to the latest info Chase had gotten, Jasmine was safe but not at her WITSEC location. Like Quentin, Jasmine had struck out on her own. Considering the recent breach in WITSEC files, that had probably kept her alive. Because Crossman would definitely want her dead since she was the one who could testify about the worst of the charges against him—murder.

Too bad April hadn't been able to move around the way that Quentin and Jasmine had, but that would have been next to impossible to do with Bailey in the hospital for two months. Plus, April probably thought she was safe.

"How did you find April in WITSEC?" Chase pressed. "Did you hack into the files?"

"Hack? That's such an ugly word. One that carries more criminal charges. No, I didn't do anything like that. Let's just say a little bird told me."

Chase silently cursed. Because that little bird could be a mole in the marshals' office.

"Why should I believe any of this?" April asked the man.

Crossman smiled again. "The week before you had your daughter, you went to the store to buy some baby things. Clothes, diapers. And a white teddy bear. From what I've been told, it had a pink bow."

Judging from how fast the color drained from April's face, Crossman was telling the truth. About that anyway. That sickened Chase to know that April and his baby were so close to danger and he hadn't even known it.

"I want to find Jasmine." Crossman inched closer to the Plexiglas. He stared at Chase. "I need to talk to her. Now, if you can arrange for that to happen, I swear to you that April and your daughter will be safe."

Chase gave him a flat look. "Even if I believed that, which I don't, I wouldn't hand over a witness to you. Besides, murder isn't the only charge against you, and April can and will help convict you of money laundering and a whole list of other crimes."

Of course, that was backup. In case the murder charges didn't put Crossman away for life. Or if he managed to wiggle out of that charge altogether. He could possibly do that if he killed Jasmine.

"Money laundering," Crossman said, his tone dismissing it. "All a misunderstanding. My lawyers can work to fix that."

"Yes, by killing my brother and me," April challenged. "By any chance, are you the one who kidnapped Quentin?"

"Interesting." Crossman made it sound as if he was hearing this for the first time. "No. But this is a sweet turn of events, wouldn't you say? I suppose there's a ransom involved? One that involves milking you for a lot of cash to pay off that pesky loan shark your brother owes?"

April didn't respond. She sighed, maybe because it was the truth.

"Do you know anything else about the kidnapping?" Chase demanded.

"Maybe," Crossman admitted. "I got a lovely visitor about a week ago. She used the name Alisha Herrington, but her real name is Renée Edmunds. She's a *friend* of Quentin's."

Oh, man. Chase had checked that visitors' log but hadn't had time to figure out if anyone on the list had been using a fake ID. "What did Renée want?"

"She offered a very interesting deal. She said she'd tell me where April was if I'd agree to leave Quentin alone."

That kicked up April's breathing a significant notch. And tightened her muscles even more.

"I told Renée I wasn't interested, of course," Crossman continued. "No reason to bargain for information I already had."

True, but there were key bits of the info that were missing. "How did Renée know where April was?"

"Maybe from that same little bird," Crossman whispered as if telling a secret. "Sometimes birds chirp to more than one person feeding them. And sometimes people chirp for a whole different reason. Like sex," he said, turning that taunting stare in April's direction.

April ignored him, and she looked at Chase. "Are we done here?"

"Yeah." Though he wasn't sure they'd actually gotten much from Crossman. Still, he needed to mull over the conversation and figure out if Crossman had revealed something he hadn't intended to reveal.

"Leaving so soon?" Crossman asked when April and Chase stood. "And here we didn't get to chat about you two getting back together. You are back together, aren't you? Have you gotten him in bed again, April?"

April shot the man another glare but didn't respond verbally. With Crossman laughing, Chase and she walked out.

"I feel like I need a bath after talking to that piece of dirt," April mumbled.

Chase knew exactly how she felt. Except the image of her taking a bath flashed through his head. Not good. Because it was yet another reminder that he couldn't allow this attraction to make him lose focus.

The moment they were in the front waiting area of the prison, Chase took out his phone to call Jericho. "I want to see if there's anything that can be done to make sure Jasmine stays safe," he explained to April. "And I can't call the marshals until we find the mole."

She nodded. "After what Crossman just said, I think he definitely has some kind of insider in either that office or one of the others."

Chase agreed, but he didn't get a chance to make that call because he saw the man making his way toward the door.

Malcolm.

"I want to talk to him," April insisted. And it didn't sound as if it would be a friendly chat, either.

Chase slipped his arm around her waist to hold her back, waiting until Malcolm had gone through the metal detector and had been searched by the guard. Chase figured even if Malcolm was armed and gunning for April that he wouldn't risk an attack here in front of the prison guard and a marshal.

"Visiting Crossman again?" April demanded the moment Malcolm had cleared security and started toward them.

Malcolm nodded. "Why are you here?" He glanced at her, then at the way Chase had his arm around her. Chase got the feeling that what Malcolm was really itching to ask was, why are you here *together*?

"We wanted to know what you discussed with Crossman on your other visits," Chase informed him. "Crossman was more than happy to tell us."

Oh, Malcolm did not like that. Suddenly, there was no pretense of being in love with April. Or even liking her. The hatred was right there in his eyes.

April folded her arms over her chest. "Let me guess. You want me to pay for your friend's murder."

"I want anyone involved to pay," Malcolm answered. But then, he huffed and some of the anger was gone. "In the beginning, I wanted you to pay. That's why I found you, but then I couldn't go through with it."

Chase had already considered that's how things had played out. Still, it cut him to the core that this man had gotten so close to April and Bailey.

"How exactly did you find me?" she asked.

His mouth tightened, and at first Chase thought Malcolm might not answer. "Crossman," he finally said. "I'm not sure, but Crossman might have also told Renée how to find you so the woman could in turn locate Quentin."

Not according to Crossman, but Chase kept that to himself. Besides, Crossman could have been lying about that. He could have indeed given any and all info to Renée if it would have helped him find Quentin and Jasmine.

Malcolm huffed. "I know how this looks with me visiting Crossman again, but I'm here to tell him to back off, that I don't want April or the baby put in danger so he can satisfy the vendetta he has against Quentin and April."

Even if he hadn't been a lawman, a comment like that would have grabbed his attention. "You know for a fact that Crossman is behind the attacks?"

"Who else would it be?" Malcolm countered, and it seemed like a genuine question. "He needs April, Quentin and that CPA out of the way, or he'll spend the rest of his life in jail."

Actually, Crossman needed only Jasmine out of the way for the murder charges, and it didn't make sense he would go through all the trouble to find April to get to Jasmine. Because there was no way the marshals would put the two women in WITSEC together.

"How'd you scramble the recordings of the conversations you had with Crossman the other times you visited him here at the prison?" Chase came out and asked.

"I don't know what you're talking about. I didn't scramble anything. Maybe Crossman paid off a guard or something?"

That was always possible, but there were handheld devices that could interfere with a signal. Visitors would be checked for that sort of thing, but someone could have slipped something like that past the guards.

Someone like Malcolm, for instance.

"I'm sorry," Malcolm said, and he aimed that apology at April. "Tina and I were close, and when I found out you could have perhaps prevented her death, I wanted to confront you, face-to-face." He glanced away. "I couldn't do that, though, after I saw how torn up you were about your baby."

Chase stared at him a long time. "Are you sure all of this isn't just to cover your tracks? Because if you helped Crossman in any way get to Bailey or April, then you'll be charged with a couple of felonies."

That renewed some of the anger on Malcolm's face. "I didn't help him." Malcolm had to get his teeth unclenched before he could continue. "Crossman murdered Tina, and he *will* pay for that." It sounded like a threat and a promise.

Chase figured he should lecture Malcolm on not taking the law into his own hands, but he seriously doubted Malcolm would listen. Besides, he didn't want to hang around here with April next to the creep who'd basically stalked her for two months.

"Come on," Chase said, and he got April moving toward the exit. However, they'd made it only a few steps when Chase's phone rang, and he saw Jericho's name on the screen.

April and he stepped to the side, and because Malcolm was still in earshot, Chase didn't put the call on speaker.

"We got a visitor," Jericho said the moment Chase answered. "You and April need to get back here right now."

Chapter Twelve

April hadn't been sure what to expect when she stepped into the Appaloosa Pass sheriff's office. All Jericho had told them on the phone was that someone had just showed up out of the blue.

That someone was Quentin.

Her brother had refused to answer any questions until she got there.

April figured that wasn't a good sign, but the fact he was there proved he hadn't faked his own kidnapping. Well, maybe it meant that.

Knowing her brother, this could be part of a sick plan, too. But at least Quentin was alive, and she got proof of that the moment Chase and she arrived. Her brother was indeed there, sitting in a chair next to one of the deputy's desks.

Quentin stood when he spotted her, but he didn't move toward her. She didn't move toward him, either. Not because she wasn't glad to see him. She was, and she was thankful he was alive. But there were so many questions, and April started with the easiest one first.

"Shouldn't you be at the hospital?" she asked.

"Trust me," Jericho said, not looking especially pleased with this development, "I tried to talk him into it."

"I'm not going back there," Quentin insisted. "But a medic came and checked my incision. I'm okay. And he left me some pain meds to take. I'll do that after we've talked."

But he sure didn't look okay. Quentin was pale and didn't seem too steady on his feet.

Chase walked to him, meeting him eye-to-eye. "Tell us about the kidnapping and how you got away."

Quentin nodded, but he didn't look at Chase. He kept his attention on April. "When I was in radiology waiting for the MRI, two armed men stormed into the room. They were both wearing ski masks so I couldn't see their faces. They forced me out of the hospital and into a van, and then they took me to a house on the edge of town."

Chase jumped right on that. He took a notepad from the deputy's desk and dropped it next to Quentin. "Write down the address of that house."

Quentin nodded, eventually. He scrawled it down and handed it to Chase. That's when she noticed Quentin was shaking. Likely caused from a combination of pain and fear.

She tried not to give in to the old tug in her heart. The one that'd coddled and protected her kid brother way too many times. The bottom line was April wasn't sure she could trust Quentin.

Jericho glanced at the address, took out his phone and stepped into his office to make the call. No doubt to get someone out there to check it out. That probably meant calling in one of the night or reserve deputies, but April was glad he wasn't going himself because it would have left just Jax, Chase and her in the office. And if her brother's kidnapping had been the real thing, then those ski mask-wearing men could come after him again.

"How did you escape?" she asked her brother.

"They had some pain meds for me there, and I spiked their coffee with them. When they fell asleep, I got out and walked here."

Chase and she exchanged glances, and he was clearly bothered by one part of that explanation, too. "The kidnappers gave you pain meds?"

Quentin nodded. "I didn't take them, though, because I knew they'd make me sleepy."

Her brother had missed the point, and April clarified it for him. "You really think Crossman or the loan shark would have cared if you were in pain?"

His eyes widened. "You believe Renée was behind the kidnapping? If she was, she didn't come to the house and the men didn't mention her."

"Did they mention anyone?" Chase snapped.

Quentin eased back down into the chair. "No. The only thing they said to me had to deal with the ransom. They said once they had the money, they'd release me."

April had no idea if that was true or not. This could still have been a ploy to draw her out. Except for those pain meds. But then, as devious as Crossman was, that might be something he'd do just to throw them off his trail.

"Renée wouldn't have put me in danger like that," Quentin added several moments later. "She's crazy, but she loves me."

"She's crazy, period," Chase corrected. "And yes, she could have put you in that kind of trouble. She could have done the same to Bailey, April, Jax and me."

Quentin made a sound as if he didn't quite buy that, and it made April wonder if Renée and her brother had indeed partnered up on this. But if so, then why had Quentin escaped?

Or had he?

"Did you get the ransom money?" Quentin asked her. "Because if you did, I need to borrow some of it."

April didn't even bother trying to choke back a groan. Chase groaned right along with her. "Did you fake all of this?" Chase came right out and asked.

That got Quentin right back on his feet. "No. Absolutely not." But the burst of energy didn't last long. "If I don't pay the money I owe, they'll kill me."

Again, April tried not to give in to the emotion that caused inside her. "How much?"

"A hundred thousand," Quentin answered after a long pause.

Less than half of what the kidnappers had demanded. Still, it was a lot of money. "How the heck did you get involved with a loan shark?" But April waved off any answer he might give her.

And he would have had an answer, all right. One that she likely wouldn't want to hear. Her brother always seemed to be involved in something messy, and criminal, like this.

"It's not like you think," Quentin insisted. "The money wasn't…" He stopped and shook his head. "You've always taken care of me. Ever since Mom and Dad were killed, you've been the one person I can rely on."

He was playing with her heartstrings now. Or maybe he was dodging the truth about why he'd borrowed that money. The ploy was something April recognized. She had indeed taken care of him, but that was about to end.

"I'll give you the money," April said. "But there are conditions attached. You'll take a polygraph, and during that test, I intend to ask you a lot of questions. If you've lied to me, about anything, then you won't get another dime of my money."

The surprise, then the anger, flared in Quentin's eyes. "How could you not trust me? I'm your brother and you claim to love me."

That was probably meant to hurt her. It didn't work. "I do love you, but I don't trust you." She didn't linger on Quentin but instead turned to Chase. "How soon can you set up a lie detector?"

"Soon," Chase assured her.

Jax made a sound of agreement. "I'll get started on that right now. I can probably have the examiner in here within an hour."

"The test could be wrong," Quentin argued. "I mean, there's a reason the results from a polygraph aren't admissible in court."

April ignored him and headed for the break room at the end of the hall. Chase followed her. She wasn't sure what his reaction would be to her demand, but he gave her a nod of approval.

"You think he'll go through with the polygraph?" Chase asked.

"He'll probably try to worm his way out of it. It won't work. Without the test, the loan shark won't get the money, and Quentin will just have to deal with the consequences himself."

Chase took her by the arm and led her to a chair. It took April a moment to realize why he'd done that. She was trembling. It wasn't just because she'd finally stood up to her brother, but an avalanche of all the things that'd happened.

"I know that wasn't easy for you," he said, handing her a cup of water.

"Quentin made it easier." She looked up at him. "He's not telling the truth about something. I just hope that something doesn't have anything to do with Bailey's kidnapping."

Judging from the hard look that put in his eyes, Chase felt the same way.

April looked up when she heard the footsteps. Not Quentin, thank goodness. It was Jericho.

"The place where Quentin claims he was held is a rental house that's supposed to be unoccupied according to the owner," Jericho explained. "I'm short on help right now so two Texas Rangers are headed out there. If they see anything, they'll bring in the CSIs to go through the place."

April figured there wouldn't be anything to find since the hired guns wouldn't have left anything incriminating behind. Still, it was all necessary since any and every little thing could perhaps help them untangle this dangerous situation.

Jericho glanced over his shoulder into the squad room, and April saw what'd gotten his attention. Quentin. He was making his way toward them. But Jericho put a stop to that.

"You can wait in the interview room," Jericho said, and he shut the door to the break room.

April made a mental note to thank Jericho for that later. "I wasn't ready to go a second round with my brother," she told Chase. "I just want to go back to the safe house so I can see Bailey."

Chase made a weary sound of agreement. "Soon."

She thought there might be a *maybe* attached to that.

And there probably was. There were hired guns on the loose, and it was highly likely there could be another attack.

"I've forgotten what normal feels like," April continued. "What with WITSEC, Bailey being premature. And all the rest of it," she added.

The next sound Chase made was a weary sigh. "Sorry, but I can't give you normal."

No. He couldn't give it to himself, either. Because soon he'd have to surrender that badge and quit being himself.

"I'm sorry," April added.

He frowned. "You've been telling me that a lot lately."

"There's no telling how many apologies I'll owe you. Unlike me, you actually have a good life you'll have to give up. I think we can both agree that my old life was a mess."

Chase didn't argue with that, but he did move closer. And he stared at her. "Your new life's also a mess."

Considering it was the truth, April was surprised that she managed a smile. Surprised, too, when Chase slipped his hand around the back of her neck and eased her to him.

No kiss, but he brushed his mouth against her temple. His arms were so warm. His breath, as well, and April just slid right into him, taking everything he was offering. Despite the consequences.

Getting close to Chase always came with a high price.

Maybe not immediately. But he'd regret this. Soon, there'd be the resentment in his eyes. Soon, the bad blood would resurface, eating away at him and making him remember all the reasons he should have never gotten involved with her in the first place.

But no high price right now. Just the warmth. Then,

the heat. Always the heat. Even though he didn't tighten his grip, she felt the attraction tug at her. Urging her to get closer and take even more from him.

He cursed, a really bad word that had her looking up at him to see if something had prompted it. Something had. *Her. This.*

April started to move away from him, but Chase held on, pinning her against the wall with his body. Now, the kiss came. The full slam of heat, too. She was certain Chase didn't actually want this, but he was just as powerless as she was when it came to this attraction.

He deepened the kiss. Mercy, did he. His mouth knew hers way too well and knew just how to coax the fire from her. Not that he had to do much coaxing. The kiss and being so close to him had already accomplished that. He robbed her of her breath, any shred of common sense, and he just kept on robbing until soon the kisses weren't enough.

April wanted more.

She wanted Chase.

And she got him. Well, more of that body-to-body contact anyway. She hooked her arms around him, pulling him closer. Not that he had far to go. They were already pressed against each other, but the slight adjustment aligned them in just the right way to have sex. It was out of the question, of course.

Still, her body got the notion that it was a done deal.

In that moment April understood why people did such stupid things. Because this was stupid. But it was also what she wanted more than anything. More than sanity. More than her next breath. The problem was she could feel the same need in Chase. Which meant they were in a boatload of trouble if one of them didn't stop.

Chase was the one to do that. Thank goodness, since April couldn't force herself away from him. But Chase let go of her and stepped back.

He didn't look at her right off. He stared at the ceiling while he mumbled profanity. And in this case, the profanity wasn't directed at her but rather at himself. Something April totally understood.

"I'm not apologizing," he finally said. He might have added more to that. Especially some more profanity, but his phone rang.

Timing was a strange thing. Because if the call had happened just a couple of minutes earlier, that kiss wouldn't have happened. Nor that non-apology. And despite the fact April knew she should regret it, she didn't. For those minutes, she'd had Chase, and even though it was only temporary, it was better than the scowls and the painful reminders of what she'd done.

"Unknown caller," Chase said when he glanced at the screen.

That took care of any of the remaining fire in her blood. April held her breath, waiting for him to answer the call and put it on speaker.

"Marshal Crockett," the woman said. "It's Renée."

Chase moved quickly, heading out of the break room and down the hall until he reached Jericho in the squad room. April was right behind him.

"Where are you, Renée?" Chase asked her. The question got Jericho's attention as it was probably meant to do.

"You know I can't tell you that because you'll arrest me." It sounded as if Renée was crying. "I can't go to jail and I can't live without Quentin." Yes, definitely crying because she made a hoarse sob. "April turned him against me."

Chase gestured for April to stay quiet before she could say anything. Probably because he thought Renée might say more if the woman believed she was talking to only him. Or maybe he just didn't want Renée to know April was with him.

"Why do you think April's turned him against you?" Chase asked Renée. "Have you spoken to Quentin?"

Silence, punctuated by more sobs. "Because why else would Quentin have left me?"

April could think of several reasons. Well, one big one anyway. Renée was crazy.

"How and when did Quentin leave you?" Chase pressed.

The next round of crying was considerably louder. "He ran away."

April heard the movement behind her, and whirled around to see her brother standing in the doorway of the interview room. Quentin had no doubt heard Renée's every word, but Chase also motioned for him to stay quiet.

"You're the one who had Quentin kidnapped?" Chase asked the woman.

"No. I didn't. I had him brought to me. But he agreed to it. He said it was a way of keeping him safe from Crossman. A way of getting the money he needed, too. And I would get to be with him."

The anger roared through April, followed by a sickening feeling in the pit of her stomach. She hadn't believed Quentin was telling her the truth, but it hurt to hear it spelled out.

Chase lifted his gaze, slowly, and he glared at Quentin. "Quentin was the one who came up with this plan?"

"I came up with it," Renée quickly volunteered. "After I made him understand all the advantages, he agreed to it."

"So, what changed?" Chase demanded. "Why did Quentin stop agreeing?"

"April must have gotten to him. Because Quentin left when I was out taking care of some things. Do you know where he is? I have to see him now. I have to convince him his sister's wrong, that I really do love him."

Part of her wanted to feel sorry for Renée, but April didn't feel anything but hatred for the woman.

"I can't stay on the line any longer," Renée said. "I don't want you tracing this and finding out where I am. Call me if you hear from Quentin."

The moment Renée hung up, April turned and faced her brother. "You lied. Again."

He nodded, his breath already gusting. "I was desperate."

"That doesn't make it all right." She wanted to scream. Or slap him. But the truth was, April should have expected exactly this from her brother. He'd done similar things time and time again.

Chase stepped closer to Quentin, and April hadn't thought it possible, but he looked just as enraged as she felt. "Why'd you *escape* from Renée? And this time everything you tell me—*everything*—had better be the truth."

Quentin nodded, swallowed hard. "I needed money so I called Renée. She was thrilled to hear from me in that stalker, obsessive kind of way. But like I said, I was desperate for the money and thought I could get it from her. She said she was into something and didn't have access to her funds."

"Into something?" April snapped. "What exactly?"

"I don't know, but after everything I've learned, maybe she was indeed behind Bailey's kidnapping. Renée might have thought she could use Bailey to find me."

April didn't doubt that, and the woman had said as much when they'd been by the creek. Plus, Renée had asked Shane for money, which meant she likely wasn't lying about not having access to her funds.

"So, Renée and you concocted that idiotic plan to have you taken from the hospital," Chase tossed out there.

Quentin's eyes widened. "Yes, but I had no idea she was going to use real gunmen. I certainly hadn't thought there'd be shots fired."

"A man died," April reminded him. "True, the guy was a hired gun and deserved it, but innocent bystanders could have been hurt. *We* could have been hurt." She motioned at Jericho, Jax and Chase.

"I didn't know until after the fact. I swear," Quentin insisted.

"What happened then?" Chase went on. "Did you have a so-called change of heart and escape from the very people who kidnapped you?"

"The gunmen were going to turn on Renée," Quentin explained. "I heard them talking after she left, and they were going to kill her, and me, once they had the ransom money."

April didn't say I told you so, but she wanted to badly. "You were a fool to trust hired guns."

Quentin nodded again, but it wasn't just regret that she saw in his eyes when their gazes met. It was something else. Determination, maybe?

"I can fix this," Quentin said to her before turning to Chase. "You want Renée and those men she hired? Then, I'll help you get them."

Chapter Thirteen

Chase was second-guessing this plan.

Yes, he wanted Renée and her thugs. Wanted answers that would put an end to the danger. But this plan put Jax and Jericho right on a collision with a crazy woman and Quentin, a man they couldn't trust.

"I should have been the one to meet with Renée," Chase said under his breath. Obviously, though, he didn't say it softly enough because April glanced at him and scowled.

"You and I have huge targets on us," she reminded him.

Something she'd mentioned several times during the planning stage of what could turn out to be a deadly trap. Because after all, if Quentin could try to turn the tables on Renée, then she could do the same to them.

It didn't help that Renée had picked a really lousy meeting place. And she'd been adamant about it, too. She had insisted on meeting Quentin at a public place with lots of people around. In other words, there was no way Jax or Jericho could control the security.

That's why Chase had wanted to nix it. His brothers and Quentin had disagreed just as adamantly. He was outnumbered, so the plan had been tweaked, then finalized, and now Jax, Jericho and Quentin were on their way to the fairgrounds, where crews were setting up for tomorrow's rodeo.

Thankfully, the tweaking had involved a slight change of venue. Instead of at the rodeo arena itself, the meeting would take place in the concession area, where there was less chance of having people wander onto the scene.

Of course, Jericho had put some of his own security in place, as well. Two Rangers and a reserve deputy had gone out ahead of them and were scoping out the fairgrounds to make sure this wasn't an ambush waiting to happen. If they got lucky, the precaution would just be overkill.

Because maybe Renée's only goal was to get her hands on Quentin.

If so, perhaps Jericho could arrest the woman and her armed *employees* before they managed to do any damage.

Chase had also made sure April was safe, too. He'd called in two of the deputies, Dexter Conway and Carlos Jimenez, to man the sheriff's office and provide backup if needed. He'd also locked the front door and set the security alarm to cover all the windows and exits. Chase hoped like the devil all of that was overkill, too.

"You look ready to jump out of your skin," Carlos said, glancing at April. "And you didn't eat hardly a bite of your dinner."

"I'm not hungry," April answered. But Carlos was right about the jumping-out-of-her-skin part. April alternated between pacing, checking the time and nibbling on her bottom lip.

Chase started to give her a mini-lecture on how she should indeed eat some of the sandwich and fries he'd ordered for her from the diner across the street. But then, he didn't have much of an appetite, either.

What had helped both of them was another quick video "chat" with Bailey. The baby had been sound asleep, but it'd been good just to see her face and to know that everything was still all right at the safe house.

"You could try to rest in the break room," Chase suggested. But he wanted to kick himself. Because judging from the surprise that flashed across her face, April was remembering those kisses they'd shared there just a few hours earlier.

Not especially what he wanted on her mind, or his, but at least she no longer looked to be on the verge of a panic attack. Too bad it didn't last. His phone rang, and April's nerves jumped right back to the surface.

He halfway expected to see Unknown Caller on the screen, but it was a name he actually recognized. Marshal Harlan McKinney. He'd not only worked with Harlan on several cases, but Chase also trusted the man.

Chase didn't put the call on speaker. Just in case this was another dose of bad news, he didn't want to send April over the edge. Still, she moved closer, where she would undoubtedly be able to hear at least some of the conversation.

"We found something," Harlan said the moment he came on the line. "There was a mole. Not a marshal, though. It was a computer tech working out of the Austin office. Her name's Janette Heller. Ring any bells?"

He had to think about it a few seconds. "No. Should it?"

"Maybe. She does background checks and such so I thought maybe you'd crossed paths with her."

"It's possible. I've had a lot on my mind lately." A huge understatement. "Has she been arrested?"

"Yeah, she's in custody. Lawyered up right away, of course, but we have what we need to set her bail sky-high. The FBI techs went through her computers, and they found enough to prove she's hacked into some WITSEC files."

"Any idea who hired her to do that?" Chase immediately asked.

"Following the advice of her lawyer, she hasn't said a word. Her lawyer's a bigwig, too. One who costs way over her standard of living."

"Maybe because she's using the money she got from hacking to pay for it?"

"Maybe." But Harlan didn't sound entirely convinced of that. "This is the kind of lawyer who has a waiting list of clients, but he dropped everything and came when she called."

So, obviously this Janette had some kind of clout or a backer who hadn't come up yet in the investigation. "You think she'll eventually talk and tell us who she's working for?"

"Not without some kind of incentive. It's my guess she won't be giving up that info unless we offer her some kind of deal. Are you okay with that, especially since it was her hack job that put April and your baby in danger?"

No, he wasn't okay with it. But Chase also wasn't okay with letting the person behind this go free, either. If it was Crossman and Janette was his "little bird," they could use this to freeze his assets and stop future attacks.

"Offer Janette the deal," Chase finally answered. "Call me if you get a name from her."

Harlan assured him he would and ended the call. Chase immediately turned to April to tell her the news.

"Thank God," she said. Obviously, she'd heard more than bits and pieces of the conversation.

Finally, he saw some of that tension drain from her, and April slipped her arms around him as if it was something she did all the time. This was a by-product of all that kissing. It'd broken down barriers.

Chase didn't go stiff, exactly, but April must have picked up on his hesitation because she pulled back. Or at least that's what she was in the process of doing, but Chase eased her right back to him. It didn't last because the movement behind him snagged Chase's attention.

Dexter walked toward the window and looked out.

"What's wrong?" Chase immediately asked the deputy.

Dexter shook his head. "I just thought I saw someone in the alley next to the diner."

Normally, that wouldn't have put Chase on edge, but there was nothing normal about this situation.

"Wait in Jericho's office," Chase told April, and he went to the front to have a look for himself.

Nothing.

"Maybe it was a shadow," Dexter added.

Maybe. But with everything else that'd happened, Chase wasn't taking any chances. He kept looking, searching for anything that was out of place.

There were people in the diner. People milling around some of the shops, too, but it would have been unusual for someone to be in that particular alley unless it was one of the diner workers on a smoke break.

The minutes crawled by, and Chase glanced over his shoulder to make sure April had gone into Jericho's office. She had, but she was peering out the doorway. When he shifted his gaze back to the alley, he saw it then.

Someone was at the back of the diner and darted out of sight. Someone dressed all in black.

Chase and Dexter drew their weapons.

"Who's out there?" April asked.

But Chase didn't get a chance to answer because he saw more movement in the alley. Not a person dressed in black, either. This was a woman, and someone he instantly recognized.

Renée.

Hell. What was she doing here?

APRIL COULDN'T SEE what'd caused Chase and Dexter's reaction. But both of them snapped back their shoulders. Chase and Dexter had already pulled their guns, but the other deputy did the same.

She tried to tamp down the fear. Tried to remind herself that this could all be just a precaution. However, it didn't feel like one.

Without taking his attention from the window, Chase took out his phone. April had no idea who he was calling, but she had no trouble hearing what he said once the person answered.

"Renée is here."

That put April's heart in her throat. Certainly the woman must have known Quentin wouldn't be here, that he was at the meeting that Renée herself had helped set up. So, what did she want?

April figured Renée hadn't come here just to chat.

Maybe they'd been wrong about Renée's obsession with Quentin. Maybe April was the woman's target.

Or...

April's stomach twisted. This could have something to do with the ransom money that would soon be delivered. April had slashed the amount to only what Quentin needed to pay off the loan shark, but what if Renée intended to take that money and use it to try to get Quentin back in her good graces?

But there was another possibility. One that April didn't like.

What if Renée and her brother were working together on this?

Chase ended his call, and with his gaze firing all around, he glanced back at her. He probably tried to give her a reassuring look. But he failed. April could practically feel the danger and his concern about it.

"Keep an eye on the roof," Chase told the deputies.

Though that order had no sooner left his mouth when April heard a sound she definitely didn't want to hear.

The alarm from the security system.

It started to scream through the building. It screamed through her, too. Because it meant someone had just broken in.

Chase ran to her, pushing her deeper into Jericho's office. "Take the gun from the top right desk drawer," he instructed. "And keep watch on the window behind you."

Her heart was already racing, but that caused it to race even more. April hurried to the desk and took out the gun. After going into WITSEC, she'd taken firearms training and knew how to shoot. She prayed, though, that it wouldn't come down to her doing that.

"The alarm was triggered from the break room," Dexter called out to them.

So close, just up the hall. There was a back door and windows in the room, but Renée must have known the sheriff's office would be wired for security.

Was it some kind of diversion?

Several moments later, the alarm stopped. No doubt because Dexter had turned it off so they could hear if anyone was actually in the building.

It was hard for April to hear much of anything with her pulse throbbing in her ears, but both Chase and Dexter had their guns aimed at the break room. She figured Carlos was watching the front in case one of Renée's hired thugs came crashing through the door. If that happened, it would be a gutsy move, an attack in broad daylight. But then, Renée hadn't exactly been predictable.

"Do you see anyone?" April risked asking.

Chase shook his head. "If someone opened the break room door, then they closed it."

The relief came. But didn't last. Because that could mean the someone had gotten inside before closing the door.

Carlos cursed, and that sent Dexter pivoting in the direction of his fellow deputy. Chase glanced at Carlos, too, and while he didn't curse, he certainly wasn't pleased about whatever he saw.

"Get down on the floor," Chase ordered her, and he stepped out. "A gunman's in the alley."

That was the only thing he managed to say before there was another sound that April didn't want to hear.

Gunshots.

Thick blasts that crashed into the front of the building.

"The windows are bullet resistant," Chase reminded her.

But he didn't return fire. Chase didn't spare more than a glance at the front. Instead, he kept his attention nailed to the break room.

And then he took aim.

Fired.

The shot rocketed through the hall, but since April was on the floor she couldn't see who Chase had shot at or if he'd hit his target.

More of those thick blasts sounded from the front. Chase fired another shot at the break room.

Then, nothing.

Everything went quiet. While April was glad the shots had stopped, she doubted that was a good thing.

"Renée's getting away," Dexter shouted. The deputy started toward the front, probably to go after her, but Chase stopped him.

"It could be a ruse to lure you out," Chase warned.

A ruse where more attackers could start pouring into the building as soon as the deputy was gone. Or else Dexter could be just gunned down by one of them.

"What about the shooter in the break room?" April asked.

"Gone, too." And Chase headed in that direction.

April wanted to shout for him to stop, that it could also be part of a ruse, but anything she said right now might be just a distraction. One that could get Chase shot. So, she waited. Breath held and praying.

It seemed to take an eternity for Chase to make his way back to her. He immediately checked on her, helping her to her feet, and he brushed a kiss on her forehead. A kiss of relief, no doubt.

"The shooter broke through the window in the break room," he explained. "But there's no sign of him or anyone else back there."

That didn't mean they wouldn't be back. Renée seemed determined to get to her.

"Why would Renée do this?" Dexter asked as Chase stepped back and took out his phone.

"Maybe for the ransom money," Chase answered, stepping back into the doorway. "Or maybe so she could kidnap April and use her to bargain with Quentin."

April hadn't even considered the last possibilities. But if Renée had thought something like that would work, she would almost certainly do it.

"Renée and her henchmen got away," Chase said to the person who answered the call he made.

It was Jericho. She recognized his voice when Chase put the call on speaker and she heard Jericho curse. "Renée must have figured out the meeting was a trap. There's not a sign of any gunmen here. We're heading back to the station now."

"Good. Because the window in the break room is broken, and I don't want to keep April here any longer than necessary."

"As soon as we get there, I'll have Jax drive with you to the safe house," Jericho assured him before he ended the call.

Finally, she'd get to be with the baby. But just as important, Chase and she would be away from another possible attack. That, in turn, might keep Jericho and the other deputies safe while they were at the office. There'd be no reason for anyone to fire into the building if she wasn't there.

"Before we leave, I'll have to check the vehicle for a tracking device," Chase reminded her. It was also a reminder that no matter how careful they were, the danger could still make its way to the safe house.

"Once Jericho makes it here, I'll do that for you," Dexter insisted. "Best if you're not out there any longer than necessary."

She agreed. Of course, that meant Dexter and anyone who went after Renée and those men were in just as much danger. It was Dexter's job, of course, but it didn't make her feel any better about it.

April just wanted all of this to end.

Chase didn't move from the doorway of Jericho's office, obviously still guarding her and still keeping watch, but he did glance back at her. He didn't try to assure her that everything would be okay. Maybe because she knew an assurance like that would be a lie. Still, she saw the shared emotions in his eyes.

The fear for their daughter.

Chase's phone rang again, and just like that her heart was right back in her throat. She prayed nothing else had gone wrong. Prayed even more when Chase didn't put the call on speaker. The only time he did that was when he wanted to shelter her from possible bad news.

Again, she waited and tried to figure out who had called and what was going on, but Chase wasn't doing any talking, only listening.

"How did that happen?" Chase asked. She couldn't hear the response, but she saw the muscles in his shoulder tighten. "You can tell me about it when you get here."

Thankfully, the conversation didn't last long. "What happened?" April asked the second he ended the call.

It took Chase a moment to gather his breath. "Quentin's missing."

Chapter Fourteen

April shook her head and continued pacing. "How could Quentin possibly go missing?" she mumbled. It wasn't really a question directed at Chase, but it was something April had been asking herself since Jericho had delivered the news fifteen minutes earlier.

Chase didn't have an answer yet.

However, the person who might have answers—Jericho—pulled to a stop in front of the sheriff's office and got out. Dexter unlocked the door for him, but Jericho paused only long enough to examine the damage to the front windows.

"Is all of this Renée's doing?" Jericho asked. Jax followed him inside.

"She was nearby," Chase settled for saying. "If we'd managed to catch her, she probably would have claimed she was in the wrong place at the wrong time."

Heck, maybe she was. There was a lot of crazy stuff going on, though, and Renée always seemed to be at the center of it.

Along with Quentin.

April went closer to Jericho as soon as he was inside. Dexter didn't come in, though. He headed toward the parking lot, probably to check to make sure no one had planted a tracking device on the vehicle they were driving back to the safe house.

"What happened to my brother?" April wanted to know.

Jericho huffed. "As we were leaving the rodeo, someone let out the bulls into the arena and then set off some firecrackers. That didn't please the bulls, and they started running around. In the chaos, Quentin disappeared."

"You didn't hear him yell for help or anything?" she pressed.

"No. But we did hear a vehicle speeding away shortly after we lost sight of him. That probably means someone was waiting for the right moment to grab him. Or else he was waiting for the right moment to escape."

Chase glanced at her, expecting to see more worry and fear on her face. But all he saw was the same frustration no doubt mirrored on his.

"Quentin knew he was going to have to face charges for faking his kidnapping," she admitted. "It's possible he set up this meeting just so he could escape."

"Yes," Chase readily agreed. "But then why did he come to the sheriff's office in the first place?"

"Maybe to make sure I was here. Or maybe he thought I'd jump to protect him."

And April certainly hadn't done that. She'd said she would give him the money, but she had also made it clear that it was the last of the funds he'd ever see from her.

"I hate to be the one to cut Quentin any slack," Jax spoke up, "but Renée could have arranged all of this. Quentin might not have called out for help because one of her henchmen might have put a gag on him or something."

That, too, was possible, but without Quentin or Renée, it was hard to know what the truth was.

Since the breach in WITSEC, Chase had given so much thought to Quentin that his head was aching. And all that thought and guessing was probably useless anyway. He'd been investigating Quentin for years and still hadn't figured out the man. It was the same for Renée, though he'd known her only a short period of time.

"Why don't you sit down," Chase said, leading April to one of the chairs. "As soon as Dexter's done, we can leave." Something they both clearly wanted to do.

But he saw something from the corner of his eye that not only had him wondering if that was going to happen, it also put him on full alert. Chase drew his gun.

That's because he saw Malcolm making a beeline toward the sheriff's office.

Great. Chase was so not in the mood to deal with that rat, and the rat wasn't alone. Shane was walking next to him. An odd couple, for sure, and it made Chase wonder what the heck they were doing there together.

"I'll frisk them," Jax volunteered, and he was ready when the two men stepped inside. Neither seemed pleased about that, and Shane especially wasn't happy when Jax took a gun from him.

"I have a permit for that," Shane insisted.

"You don't have a permit to carry it inside here," Jax insisted right back. He went to his desk to put the gun away and to make a phone call.

Malcolm's attention went to April. Then, it snapped to Chase. "I want you to call off your dogs."

Chase just gave him a flat look. "Am I supposed to know what that means?"

Judging from the sour expression on Malcolm's face, he did expect it. "Someone's been following me since I left the prison. Following Shane, too. We figured it was some of your law enforcement buddies."

"Well, you figured wrong," Chase set them straight. He pointed to each of them. "How do you two know each other?"

"I'm trying to clear my name since you're treating me like a suspect," Malcolm snarled. "To do that, I contacted Shane to see if I could speak with Renée. But he doesn't know where she is."

Chase turned to Shane to see what he had to say about that, and Shane nodded. "I haven't found her yet, and if I had, I would have turned her in to you. She needs to be back on her meds. She needs to be in a psychiatric hospital. If she doesn't get help, she could be killed."

He couldn't argue with that. Renée needed both. But first, they had to find her.

"We spotted her here in town less than a half hour ago," Chase explained. "Either of you know anything about that?"

Both men shook their heads, but Malcolm looked considerably more alarmed by that than Shane. Was that because he'd manipulated Renée in some way, maybe to get revenge against Quentin, and the plan had backfired? Too bad Chase couldn't hook all of them up to a lie detector.

Dexter came back in, but he didn't go far once he spotted their visitors. He stayed in the doorway, his attention volleying between them and the parking lot. No doubt so he could keep an eye on the vehicle he'd just checked out for them.

Chase turned to Jericho. "Can you handle these two? I want to get April out of here."

Jericho nodded, snagged Malcolm and Shane's attention. "You two, go to the interview room. We'll finish up there."

Shane readily complied, but for a moment Chase thought Malcolm was going to come up with an excuse to leave. He didn't, though. After saying something under his breath that Chase didn't bother to hear, Malcolm went up the hall toward the interview room.

Jericho waited until they were inside before he turned to Dexter. "Did you check the unmarked squad car?" he asked.

Dexter nodded. "The truck, too. There's nothing on either of them."

"Then go ahead and drive the car to the front of the building." Jericho gave Jax, April and Chase each a glance. "You ready to go?"

Chase was more than ready, but he kept April back when Dexter hurried back to the parking lot. He didn't want April outside any longer than necessary.

"I'll be back after I drop them off," Jax told Jericho. "We can search for Quentin and Renée then."

Chase wished he could help with that. Wished even more that he could find them. But this wasn't a safe place for April to be. The shot-up windows were proof of that.

Finally, Dexter brought the black four-door car to a stop directly behind Jericho's cruiser, and Chase was ready to get April moving.

But his phone rang.

Since any and all calls could be critical, he took out his phone and saw Marshal Harlan McKinney's name on the screen. Maybe the mole, Janette Heller, had spilled her guts after getting that plea deal.

"Please tell me you have the name of the person who hired Janette," Chase greeted when he took the call.

"No. She's still negotiating the plea deal. But that's not why I'm calling." Harlan paused. "Chase, there's been a murder."

APRIL HAD SEEN Harlan's name on Chase's phone screen, but she hadn't been able to hear any of what the marshal had said that could put the thunderstruck expression on Chase's face.

"A murder?" Chase asked. "Who?"

No. Her thoughts automatically went in a bad direction. Was her brother dead? She tried to brace herself, but that was impossible. As bad as things were between Quentin and her, she hated to think of someone murdering him.

"Call me back the second you know anything," Chase said several moments later. He hung up and looked at her. "It's not Quentin. It's Tony Crossman."

Of all the names she expected to hear Chase say, that wasn't one of them. "Crossman?" Jericho and she said in unison.

Chase nodded. "He's dead."

April sank down into the nearest chair. For months, Crossman had been a bogeyman for her. A killer who wanted Quentin and her dead. And he was the reason they were in WITSEC.

Now someone had killed the killer.

"This changes everything," she said, looking up at Chase.

Another nod from Chase, and he helped her back to her feet. "We should go. It'll be getting dark soon, and it'll be harder to see if anyone tries to follow us to the safe house."

He was right, of course, and somehow April managed to get her feet moving. Hard to do, though. She felt numb. Relieved, too.

At least April felt that way until Chase ushered her out. Both Jax and he drew their weapons before they hurried her to the unmarked cruiser. Dexter and Jericho kept watch—just in case they were attacked again. That's when a big chunk of her relief vanished. Because while Crossman's death did indeed change everything, it didn't necessarily put an end to the danger.

Chase maneuvered her in the backseat of the car with him. Jax got behind the wheel, and he didn't waste any time driving them away from there.

"What happened to Crossman?" she asked, though April wasn't sure she actually wanted to hear the details. She already had way too many memories and details of murder and violence.

"He was shanked in a prison fight about an hour ago," Chase explained. "Crossman died before the medic even got to him."

"They're sure he's dead?" she pressed. "Because this could be another of his sick games." However, she couldn't imagine what Crossman would hope to gain from something like this.

She must have started to look a little panicked because Chase slipped his arm around her. "He's dead. The guards are questioning the other inmates now, but no one is jumping to take credit for it. Harlan did say the guards were surprised, though, because the other inmates actually seemed to like Crossman."

Hard to believe that he was well liked by anyone, but Crossman was a rich man, so maybe he was buying protection and favors from his fellow prisoners. After all,

Crossman had been behind bars for six months, and there hadn't been even a hint of violence directed at him.

That reminder caused everything inside her to go still.

"Malcolm was at the jail earlier today," April said. "Maybe he's the one who arranged the murder. And Crossman did hint that Malcolm had something to do with the attacks against us and Bailey's kidnapping."

"The guards will look into that." Since Chase didn't hesitate with his answer, it meant he'd already given it some thought. "They'll look into the other suspects, too," he added.

That hung in the air for several seconds. "You mean my brother."

Chase lifted his shoulder. "Quentin had reason to want Crossman dead. Renée, too, since she knew Crossman was a potential threat to Quentin."

"True, and Renée did visit Crossman at the prison, but Quentin doesn't have the money to pay for an attack like that."

"He would have if he'd gotten the money from a loan shark," Chase quickly pointed out.

April touched her fingers to her throat. Then nodded. "Quentin was evasive about why he'd borrowed that money. But why wouldn't he have just told me if he'd done that?"

Chase gave her a flat look that she had no trouble seeing even in the dim light. "It'd be like confessing to murder. And it wouldn't matter that Crossman is scum. Murder is still murder."

Yes. It sickened her to think that Quentin might have gone this far. Crossman had been a genuine threat, but he would have been convicted. Would have ended up behind bars for the rest of his life. Of course, his conviction wouldn't have ended Quentin's and her life sentences. Because they would have had to remain in WITSEC as long as Crossman was alive.

"Don't focus just on your brother," Chase said to her a moment later. "There also might have been a dispute the guards didn't know about. In other words, this might not be connected to what's happening with us."

April hoped he was right. Having Crossman dead wasn't any big loss, but she didn't want his murder on her brother's hands.

Chase maneuvered her into the crook of his arm. "Why don't you try to get some rest? It'll take us hours to get to the safe house because Jax will have to drive around a long time to make sure we aren't being followed."

April was certain that rest was the last thing she'd get, but it was no hardship to be in Chase's arms. Of course, he wasn't resting, either. His gaze was firing all around them, probably looking for more of those hired thugs.

"What if all the gunmen were working for Crossman?" she asked. If so, that meant the danger was really over.

"We'll know soon enough." Chase idly brushed a kiss on the top of her head. That, too, was no hardship, and April wondered if Chase even realized the effect he had on her.

She didn't want to hope too much that Bailey and the rest of them would all finally be safe. But the hope came anyway. No danger. No WITSEC. She could live a normal life, and Chase wouldn't have to give up his badge and family.

The thought stopped in her head.

But that would mean things would change between Chase and her. They weren't exactly riding off into the sunset together, but they had eased some of that bad blood. Being in his arms proved that. So did all those hot kisses. However, if there was no reason for them to be in hiding together, that might also give Chase a reason for them not to be together at all.

Get a grip.

If the danger had already ended, that's all that mattered. And she couldn't lose Chase because he wasn't hers to lose. Though it did feel as if someone had just crushed her heart.

Chase's phone rang, getting everyone's attention in the car, and when April saw that it was Harlan calling again, she braced herself in case he was about to name her brother as Crossman's killer.

Thankfully, Chase put the call on speaker. "Did you find out anything else about Crossman?" Chase asked.

"Not yet, but there are a few inmates who seem to want to talk. In exchange for lighter sentences, of course. Something might pan out with that, but it's not the reason I'm calling. It's about Janette."

It took April a moment to remember that was the name of the mole they'd found in the marshals' office.

"Janette took the plea deal," Harlan continued a moment later. "And she gave us the name of the person who hired her to hack into WITSEC files."

Chapter Fifteen

Renée.

Chase wasn't exactly surprised that Renée had been the one to pay off Janette, the hacker. It'd been clear from the start that the woman would do anything to find Quentin. What was surprising though was that she hadn't covered her tracks better.

Most criminals would have used a middleman to broker the deal and added layer after layer of cover so that nothing could be traced back to them. Renée hadn't done that. Why?

That'd been the question on Chase's mind during the entire drive to the safe house. And it was still on his mind now.

The safe house was quiet with Levi and Mack asleep in the living room and Jax's return to the sheriff's office. Bailey was also sleeping in the makeshift nursery they'd made out of the second bedroom, and April was in the only other bedroom across the hall. Probably to give him some alone time with Bailey.

Alone time with his thoughts, too.

So much had gone on what with the attacks, Crossman's murder and now the news about Renée hiring Janette. All of it was twisted into a tangled mess, and even the quiet didn't help Chase sort through it.

What did help was knowing that Bailey and April were safe. For now, anyway. With Crossman out of the picture, Chase had to work on keeping it that way. That started with figuring out how Renée played into all of this. Whoever was behind this wanted April hurt.

Or dead.

If it was Quentin, it could be for whatever part of April's estate he'd inherit. If it was Malcolm, it could be simple revenge. Revenge that he'd perhaps already started by having Crossman murdered. But what would Renée possibly hope to gain by killing April?

Unless…

"What's bothering you?" April asked, snapping him right out of his thoughts.

Chase looked up at her. She was in the doorway, her hands bracketed on each side of the jamb, and she was watching him watch a sleeping Bailey.

He did a double take. Because April wasn't wearing any clothes. Well, she had on a bathrobe, but that was it. Judging from the towel she had draped over her arm, she was headed to the shower.

April did her own double take when she noticed where his attention had drifted. To her body. He quickly fixed that and turned back to the baby.

"Is something wrong?" April pressed.

Because something might indeed be wrong and since he didn't want to wake Bailey, Chase stepped away from the crib and joined April in the hall so they could talk. He reminded certain parts of himself that this was just for a chat. And not so he could keep gawking at her in that bathrobe.

"I'm thinking it's possible Janette was paid to say that Renée had been the one to hire her," Chase tossed out there.

April stayed quiet a moment, obviously processing that. "Is there anything specific that makes you think that?"

"Harlan said Janette got a top-notch lawyer, one that she wouldn't normally be able to afford."

She shrugged. "Maybe Renée paid for that, too."

"That's what I thought at first, but why wouldn't Renée just spend that money to better cover up what she'd done? There doesn't appear to be a personal connection between Renée and Janette, so I'm surprised Renée didn't just put up a front man to hire her and then let Janette hang if she got caught."

April made a sound of agreement. "Especially since Renée got the information she wanted—my location so she could use Bailey and me to help her find Quentin." She paused. "So, you're thinking Malcolm could be behind this?"

"Or Quentin." Chase didn't have to wait long for the surprise to appear on April's face.

"Quentin might have needed to find you so he could get the money to pay off his debts. After all, you had a do-not-contact order on him when you entered WITSEC, and he had no way of getting in touch with you."

"Only because I thought it was too risky for us to try to communicate with each other."

Chase nodded. "So, this might have been Quentin's only way of finding you. And then he could get rid of Renée by having Janette say that Renée was the one who hired her."

"You really think so?" she asked.

Obviously, he hadn't convinced her. Chase hadn't actually convinced himself, either, but he wanted to tell her what was on his mind and hope that she could see any flaws in his theory. Because it would be a lot better for April if her brother didn't want her dead.

"Think it through," Chase continued. "Yes, Renée resents you because she believes you turned Quentin against her, but Quentin could be manipulating that. He could be baiting Renée to go after you."

April groaned, leaned against the wall. And she blinked back some tears. "I know I shouldn't be shocked by anything he's capable of doing, but it still hurts."

Now he had convinced her. But maybe he was wrong.

"I know. I'm sorry. And this is all just a theory. Quentin might be innocent." Of this, anyway.

Even though it was a different kind of dangerous to get closer to her, Chase did it anyway. He pulled her to him. And he had to give those parts of his body yet another reminder that this was a hug of comfort. Too bad those parts couldn't tell the difference.

And April felt the difference.

She eased back, looked up at him, and he saw the questions—and the heat—in her eyes.

Not good. Chase moved away from her. It didn't help. He could still feel her in his arms. Still had the taste of her in his mouth.

Still wanted her more than his next breath.

"All right." April sounded disappointed that he hadn't acted on the heat crackling between them. She fluttered her fingers toward the bathroom just up the hall. "I won't be long, and then I'll probably spend the night in here with Bailey."

Chase wanted to remind her there was a baby monitor so she could sleep in the room set up for her and still hear Bailey. Heck, he also wanted to follow April and…

Well, he wanted to have sex with her.

That was the down and dirty, but considering everything that'd gone on between them, she might turn him down flat.

His stupid body seemed to take that as a challenge. Chase grabbed the baby monitor and headed for the bathroom. She'd already turned on the shower. He could hear the water running, which meant she'd likely already stripped down.

His body took that as a challenge, too.

He knocked once, just a sharp rap, and April opened the door. He stepped inside with her and set the baby monitor on the vanity.

April stared at him. Frozen. Well, except for her breath. It was gusting.

Chase had a big reason to keep his hands off her. April was a criminal. He was a marshal. Opposites. But that didn't seem to matter when it came to this attraction between them.

It sure didn't matter now.

There were times when he wished he'd never met her. Other times when he knew he'd never have this feeling with anyone else. Despite that whole opposite thing, his feelings for her ran hot and deep. And not just sex, either.

It would have been so much simpler if this were just about sex.

"I'm never sure what I should do when it comes to

you," she said, her voice all mixed up with that gusting breath.

"I know exactly what to do with you."

And he did. Chase proved it by sliding his hand around the back of her neck and hauling her to him. His brain sent up a red flag warning. Which he ignored and kissed her.

There it was. That slam of fire that he always got whenever he was near her. He put her body right against his. Her breasts against his chest. The rest of them aligned just right, too.

She tasted like something forbidden. Probably not too far off the mark. But there was something else, as well. Something familiar that whispered of home. And family. That was brief, though, because soon the fire had its way, and his body urged him to do more than just kiss her.

So, Chase did.

He pushed the robe off her, and he lowered his mouth to her breasts. She was curvier than she had been before the pregnancy. He approved and savored every inch of her breasts until she was breathless and clutching onto him.

And kissing him in return.

April sank to the floor, pulling him down with her. It was warm and steamy like the rest of the room, and they landed on the thick bath mat. She located his mouth again and did some damage there while she went after his shirt. Once it was off, he felt her bare skin against his. Not just her breasts, either.

She was naked.

And beautiful.

Man, she knew how to take away his breath, too.

Chase considered scooping her up and taking her into

the bedroom. *Briefly* considered it. But the bedroom suddenly seemed miles away.

Their other time together had been crazy and rushed. This time was no different, and even though he wanted to slow down, to savor her a while, he knew that was a pipe dream. The need pushed aside the foreplay.

Without breaking the kiss, she fought with his jeans and would have lost that battle on her own if Chase hadn't helped. His boots, holster and the rest of his clothes went flying over the small bathroom. At the last second, he remembered to take a condom from his wallet.

And then it was his turn to freeze.

"Is it okay if we do this?" Something he should have asked before he even started this.

She blinked, and then he saw the realization hit her. "You mean because I had a baby?" Relief washed over her face, and she pulled him right back to her. "It's been two months. This is fine. Better than fine," she added in a rough whisper.

Chase had to agree with that. It was much, much better than just fine.

Despite her assurance that all was well, Chase forced himself to be gentle when he entered her. The gentleness didn't last, though. April hooked her legs around him and forced him in deeper. Harder.

Then, faster.

Even though the need was in control now, Chase still looked at her. Savoring as much of this as he could. Hanging on to every second with her.

But it didn't last.

He knew it wouldn't. The thrusts inside her took them to the exact place that fire demanded they go. April made a soft sound of pure pleasure as the climax rippled through her. It was the sound, that look on her face, the way her body gripped his. All of that took hold of him. And didn't let go.

Chase gave in to it, in to her and finished what April and he had started.

Chapter Sixteen

April figured this was as close to perfect as her life could get. Sex with Chase. Great sex at that. They had a healthy baby girl. And Crossman was dead. But even with all the semiperfectness, something big was missing.

Chase himself.

He was there physically in bed with her at the safe house, but somewhere between the time they'd made love on the bathroom floor and then come into the bedroom after Bailey's late-night feeding, he'd taken a mental hike. And it wasn't just because he'd been asleep, either. He'd likely dozed through the night, but every time April had checked, he was awake, staring up at the ceiling.

Did he regret what they'd done?

No doubt. April was pretty sure he trusted her now, but there'd always be that divide between them. A divide that even the danger, Bailey and the sex hadn't been able to erase.

Of course, it might also have something to do with the two phone calls Chase had made during the night. From what she'd been able to gather, they'd been updates from Jericho. Or rather lack of updates since there'd been no new information about the investigation.

"Want to talk about it?" she risked asking.

Even though he was still wide awake, her question seemed to startle him, and it took a moment for him to turn his head and look at her. There wasn't regret in his eyes, but there was something.

"I'm not going to apologize for what happened," he said.

All right, so maybe he wasn't as distant as she'd originally thought. "I don't want an apology. If you hadn't come into that bathroom after me, I would have made my way back to you."

In fact, she had indeed been reaching for the doorknob when she'd heard Chase's well-timed knock.

"So, what's bothering you?" she pressed even though April wasn't sure she wanted to hear what had caused his forehead to bunch up like that.

"Today is Deanne's funeral," he tossed out there.

Oh. That. She certainly hadn't forgotten about it and felt a pang of a different kind. Grief. It was so senseless that Deanne had died. Even more senseless that they still didn't know who had hired the man who'd murdered her.

"Deanne didn't have a next of kin," Chase went on, "so Jericho arranged to have her buried at the church near the ranch. We have lots of family graves there that we maintain. We'll do the same for Deanne."

April had to tamp down the lump in her throat before she could speak. "Thank you for that."

"It was all Jericho's doing. He might act like a badass, but he's got a couple of soft spots."

She'd yet to see those soft spots, but Jericho had done his best to keep Bailey and her safe, and that was plenty enough for April.

There was a sound from the baby monitor. Not a cry exactly, but Bailey was stirring. She'd had a bottle only three hours earlier so probably wouldn't be hungry yet, but she might want some attention.

"I'll get her," Chase said, dropping a kiss on her mouth before he climbed out of bed.

He was already wearing his jeans. He'd put them back on shortly after returning to the bedroom and had slept in them. With his gun and boots nearby. Reminders that even though they were in the safe house, Chase was still on alert.

With good reason.

It was entirely possible the danger wasn't over.

Also entirely possible the danger wasn't going away anytime soon. Well, unless they did something to bring things to a head.

Chase came back in the room, holding Bailey and smiling at her. For a couple of moments, the thoughts of danger and fear vanished, and April went back into that near-perfect state. This was what normal couples had.

Not that their relationship was anywhere near normal.

Still, it was nice to think of what could be.

Chase sat on the bed, easing Bailey between them. The baby volleyed glances between them as if trying to figure out what was going on. April was trying to do the same thing. However, any plans or thoughts for their future meant getting rid of one big obstacle: the person who'd set all this danger in motion.

April wanted to believe Crossman had been the one to do that, but her gut was telling her otherwise. They had to know for sure.

"We could set a trap," April tossed out there, hoping Chase didn't nix the idea before she could even explain it.

He didn't.

"I know a trap might not even be necessary," she continued. "Maybe Crossman was the only one behind all of this, but if he wasn't, then the person responsible will still want to come after me."

And that person could be Renée, Malcolm or, yes, Quentin.

Chase nodded. "I was thinking about going to Deanne's funeral in the hopes of drawing out Quentin or Renée."

She shook her head. "You're not the target. I am. The only way it would work is for me to be there."

Now he shook his head. "Too dangerous."

"It's too dangerous not to do anything. And think of what it would mean to bring this all to an end. No WITSEC. You wouldn't have to leave your family or give up your badge. Bailey could have a normal life."

Chase wasn't surprised with any part of her argument. He'd likely gone over this too many times during the sleepless night he'd just had. But he still didn't jump to agree with her that this was the fastest way.

Bailey smiled, getting their attention. The conversation was way too dark, considering they had their precious baby next to them. But it was because of Bailey that something had to be done.

"You said the funeral would be at a church near the ranch," April went on. "How hard would it be to secure the location?"

"Hard." Chase lifted his head, his gaze meeting hers. "But not impossible. The church and adjacent cemetery are in a clearing with a road in front and pastures on the back and east side. It's the west side that would pose the biggest risk. There are plenty of trees where snipers could hide."

Obviously, he'd already given this some thought.

"Even if we caught a sniper, he might not talk and tell us who hired him," she admitted.

"Yeah, and that's why I don't think this is a good idea. Too big of a risk with little chance of a payoff."

"What if the culprit thinks he or she can personally get to me?" April suggested. "Just hear me out," she added when he started shaking his head again. "We put out the word that I found something to ID the person. No specifics, only that Crossman gave me some information when we visited him right before he died."

At least Chase didn't shake his head at that. "What kind of info?"

She shrugged. "Bank routing numbers maybe that could be traced back to the person who hired those gunmen. We could say that I'm not willing to share the info with the cops yet because I want to use it as a bargaining tool to get Quentin out of hot water."

Something she'd done with the last plea deal. And she'd been getting Quentin out of hot water most of his life.

"Then what?" Chase asked. "The person responsible tries to gun you down when a sniper can't?"

The thought of that required her to take a deep breath. "Maybe no guns will be involved at all. I could stay inside the church the whole time. Both Quentin and Renée are fugitives. If they try to get inside to see me, you can arrest them. Interrogate them. And maybe get them to crack."

Which shouldn't be hard in Renée's case. Her short fuse and mental instability might be enough to get a confession.

"What if it's Malcolm?" Chase snapped. "I don't have any grounds to arrest him—yet."

"No. But if he shows up, I can tell him Crossman gave me proof that he's the one behind the attacks. If Malcolm is indeed the one behind this, I think he'll have some kind of reaction to that."

"A bad reaction," Chase pointed out.

"And if it is, you'll arrest him."

"What if he attacks first?" he pressed.

"Then you'll stop him. We can add some urgency to all of this by saying after the funeral I'll be heading back to WITSEC. And meeting with the marshals to tell them everything I supposedly learned from Crossman because I've worked out the plea deal for Quentin to take his false kidnapping and extortion charges off the table."

Chase looked as if he wanted to curse. Hard to do that with a still-smiling baby between them. "I don't want you in that kind of danger."

"I'm already in that kind of danger," she reminded him. "And if the suspects don't show up, at least I get to say my goodbyes to Deanne."

Still, no response from Chase.

"Please," April pressed. "Call Jericho and let's set this up. Levi and Mack could stay here with Bailey, and in just a few hours this could all be over."

He didn't exactly jump to take out his phone, and she could see the wheels practically turning in his head. It wasn't a perfect plan. Far from it. However, she felt in her gut that one way or another it would bring all of this to a close.

"I won't make you regret this," she added.

"I already do," he said.

But Chase reached for his phone to make the call.

EVERYTHING WAS QUIET. Too quiet, maybe. Of course, if it hadn't been quiet, Chase would have still felt the same uneasiness.

And had the same doubts about this so-called plan.

Having April out in public like this could turn out to be deadly. But then again, having her anywhere could have the same consequences. After all, someone—maybe Renée—had tried to kidnap April from the sheriff's office in broad daylight. The woman certainly wouldn't have any trouble showing up at a country church.

Nor would any thugs she might have hired to finish off April.

That's why Chase had insisted on April wearing a Kevlar vest under her shirt. She could still be injured in an attack, but the vest was something at least. The church had also been searched from top to bottom.

Of course, there were plenty of places for an attacker to hide a bomb or some other kind of device in an old church like this, especially since Deanne's funeral arrangements had been made before this plan had been put into motion. Someone could have easily gotten into the church. Still, they'd done all they could in that particular area of security.

As a final part of this plan, April was also armed. Everyone in or near the church was since, with the exception of April, they were all lawmen.

Jericho, Jax, Carlos and Dexter.

No minister. Chase hadn't wanted to bring Reverend Marcum into the middle of this. And the burial crew wouldn't show up until April was away from the grounds. That would ensure the crew's and minister's safety.

Too bad Chase couldn't do much of anything else to give April that same kind of assurance.

Or comfort.

April had started crying the moment they'd stepped into the church for the closed-casket funeral. And she was still fighting the tears now while they stood in the back corner. Where they would stay to see how this plan played out.

The corner wasn't ideal since the walls of the church were wood, but it was away from any doors and windows, and it gave Chase the vantage point of being able to see both the front and rear exits while keeping April right next to him.

She was still looking shaky and had a death grip on the small bouquet of flowers she was holding. Flowers that Jax had remembered to pick up for her so April would have something to put on Deanne's coffin. Chase hadn't expected his brothers to be so accommodating to April, but he was thankful for it. Thankful, too, that they were putting their lives on the line for this.

"Deanne's death wasn't your fault, you know," Chase told her when the tears started again. But he was repeating himself, and April didn't look as if she believed him any more now than the first time he'd said it.

"If it hadn't been for Deanne, we might not have gotten Bailey back." She whispered it as if it were too frightening to say it aloud.

Chase shared that same frightening realization with her. Thank God they'd managed to get to Bailey because as bad as this all was—and it was *bad*—at least their baby was safe.

The challenge would be to keep it that way.

There was some movement near the front door, and Chase automatically stepped in front of April. But it was only Jericho, and his brother made a sweeping glance around before he made his way to them.

"Anything yet?" Chase asked.

Jericho shook his head. "No sign of snipers or anyone

else for that matter. But then, I wasn't convinced any of our three suspects or their hired guns would just come waltzing up to the place."

"They might if they believe this is their last chance to get to me," April reminded him. "Did the word get out that I'm about to leave for good?"

"It did. We used Janette for that."

Chase pulled back his shoulders. "The hacker who broke into WITSEC files? You trust her to do something like that?"

"I don't trust her one bit, but trust has nothing to do with this. As part of her plea deal, she told us that she communicated with Renée or whoever hired her by transferring the info she hacked into an encrypted file that she then put in an online chat room."

April jumped right on that. "You're not sure it was actually Renée who hired her?"

"Not sure of much of anything, and I don't think Janette is, either. It's fairly easy to pretend to be someone else on the internet. And I have to wonder—why would Renée let this be traced back to her?"

Chase had asked himself the same thing, and he didn't like the answer any more than the uneasy feeling in the pit of his stomach. Yes, Renée could have just screwed up. She was crazy after all. But it would have been just as easy for someone to frame her.

Either Malcolm or Quentin.

"Anyway," Jericho continued, "the marshals used the same encryption code and put out the news about April heading back to WITSEC today."

"But won't our suspects know the info didn't come from Janette?" Chase asked.

Jericho gave him a half smile. "It did come from her.

That was another part of the plea deal we worked out with Janette. They allowed her to log on to a computer but watched everything she was doing to make sure she didn't try to double-cross us."

April didn't seem that relieved. "What if Janette found a way around that? What if she figured out a way to tell her boss that this was a trap?"

"Then the bad guy or woman doesn't show up," Jericho explained, looking at Chase. "Which might turn out to be a good thing. If we don't catch him or her today, we'll keep looking, and maybe you won't have to be in WITSEC that long."

Maybe. But any amount of time was too long to be without his badge. Still, it was better than any other alternative Chase had managed to come up with.

Jericho checked his watch. "How much time are we going to give this to play out?"

Chase wanted to say not much time at all, but the look in April's eyes begged him to wait. "Let's give it another ten minutes."

That didn't please either Jericho or April. His brother wanted to wrap this up now, and April had probably been ready to stand there for the rest of the day despite only the thin possibility of ending all of this.

"I'll tell the others," Jericho said, heading back out the door.

April turned to him the moment Jericho was gone. "I'm sorry. I really hoped this would work."

Chase didn't tell her that no apology was needed. Instead, he brushed a kiss on her cheek.

She glanced at the casket at the front of the church. "Deanne deserved better than this."

Yes, she did. Despite the fact they'd put out the word

in the town newspaper about the funeral service, there'd
been no visitors. Too bad.

"I think Deanne would have been pleased, though,
that we're using her funeral to draw out the person responsible for her murder," Chase added.

April nodded. Gave a heavy sigh. And looked at the
casket again. "I want to say goodbye to her, and then we
can get ready to leave."

Chase was relieved about the leaving part, but he
wasn't too happy about her being in the front of the
church. It put her way too close to the windows and back
exit. Still, he couldn't deny her this.

"Just make it fast," he insisted.

He drew his gun and kept watch all around them,
though he knew if a gunman tried to get past Jericho and
the others that he'd hear the commotion before anyone
actually made it into the church.

That left the windows.

There were lots of them. A dozen, but they were all
stained glass, making it impossible to see through them.
However, if a sniper had indeed managed to get close
enough, he could use an infrared device to pinpoint
April's exact location. That was the main reason Chase
had to keep her away from them.

Thankfully, April did hurry. She went to the front of
the church, Chase was right by her side, and she placed
the flowers on Deanne's coffin.

"Thank you," April whispered to the woman. "I swear,
I'll do everything I can to make this right."

Chase didn't especially like that promise. He'd hoped
this would be the last of April sticking her neck out there.
That didn't mean he wouldn't be doing the same thing.
He wanted this person caught and punished.

April paused, her mouth moving, but Chase couldn't tell what she was saying. A prayer, maybe. It lasted only a few moments before she turned to him, obviously ready to go.

Chase didn't waste any time. He got her moving toward the front entrance, where they'd left the unmarked cruiser. Of course, this was the most dangerous part.

With April out in the open.

There were only six steps leading down from the church and only about a dozen more steps to the car, but it would almost certainly feel like an eternity.

He stopped once they reached the door, and Chase looked out to get a signal from Jericho that it was okay to move April. His brother made a sweeping look around, gave him a nod, and he opened the door for them.

Chase took a deep breath, ready to move, but before he could do anything else, the worst happened.

A blast tore through the church.

Chapter Seventeen

The sound was deafening, and April wasn't sure what the heck had caused it.

Chase seemed to know what was going on, though, because he hooked his arm around her and bolted out of the building and onto the landing just outside the front door.

April saw Jericho and the others then. Jericho and Jax were scrambling around and taking cover on the side of the unmarked cruiser that Chase and she had used to get there. Dexter and Carlos hurried behind Dexter's truck. Thankfully, none of them seemed to be hurt.

Maybe it would stay that way.

She glanced over her shoulder and saw the damage inside. Someone had obviously set off some kind of explosive, and the blast had ripped through the center of the church, splintering the pews and scattering debris everywhere. Chunks of the ceiling were falling, some landing on Deanne's coffin.

Who had done this?

And how had they managed it?

The building had been checked and double-checked. And Jericho and the other deputies had patrolled the grounds the entire time Chase and she had been inside.

There was no way someone could have gotten past them to do this. Unless someone had managed to shoot a long-range explosive.

"We need to get in the car," Chase insisted.

With his body practically wrapped around hers and with his gun drawn, Chase started for the steps that led down to the flagstone walkway. But they didn't get far.

Before the shot rang out.

Quickly followed by a second and a third one.

Cursing, Chase yanked her back into the entry just as one of the bullets slammed into the doorjamb where they'd just been.

Her heart was going a mile a minute. The bad thoughts, too. Someone was shooting at them. Maybe someone who'd used the explosion as a distraction to get closer to fire those bullets.

April grabbed the gun from her purse and dropped the purse onto the floor. No need for it now, and she wanted to free up her hands in case she got the chance to return fire.

Or if she had to fight back.

That didn't help settle any of her nerves and fear.

There was a loud noise behind her, and for one terrifying moment, April thought maybe someone had sneaked in through the back and had shot at them. But it wasn't a bullet. Another piece of the ceiling had fallen. Worse, it looked as if the whole place was ready to collapse.

"We can't stay here," April managed to say.

Chase made a sound of agreement, his gaze zooming all around. The only other one of the lawmen whom she could actually see now was Jericho, and he was pinned down on the side of the cruiser, and someone was shooting at him.

That's when April realized there was more than one gunman.

Another part of the ceiling fell, crashing to the floor directly behind them. It was obvious they didn't have many options, but one of those options definitely wasn't to stay put.

"We'll jump off the side of the steps," Chase finally said, tipping his head in that direction. "Move fast and get down the second we're on the ground."

She nodded, but that was all April had time to do before Chase latched on to her arm and got them running. The bullets didn't stop coming, and she could have sworn it took hours for them to maneuver the short distance.

The steps were wide, at least ten feet across, and the moment they reached the side, Chase and she dropped to the ground, landing in the flower bed that stretched across the entire side of the church. All things considered, it wasn't the worst place to be since the steps were made of concrete and flagstone.

But Jericho and Jax didn't have that kind of protection.

They and the other deputies were pinned down, and the bulk of the bullets seemed to be aimed at them.

"Do you see the shooters?" Chase called out to them.

"They sped up in a black car the same time as the explosion," Jericho answered. "They're blocking the road. Two of them. Maybe more."

April thought her heart had skipped a beat. Maybe more wasn't good, and with the explosive and the gunfire, it was possible other shooters were getting in place to come at them from all angles.

Chase glanced back at her, probably to make sure she

hadn't been hurt by any of the falling debris or bullets. She hadn't been, but there was a cut above Chase's left eyebrow. Not serious. However, it was a reminder that this could have been a whole lot worse.

And still might be.

"I'll get in the car and will pull it over to you," Jericho said.

It was a possible way out. But it wasn't without risks.

When Jericho levered himself up to open the door, the shots came even faster, tearing into the vehicle. It was bullet resistant, but that didn't mean the bullets wouldn't get through. And the shooters were doing their best to tear through the engine. No doubt so they could disable it since it was the nearest vehicle to Chase and her.

April watched, her breath stalled in her throat, as Jericho opened the driver's side door. Jax did the same to the back. Jericho didn't have the keys, Chase did, but she was hoping once he got inside, it wouldn't take him long to hotwire the car and drive to them.

Of course, that wouldn't solve their problem of the road being blocked, but it was a start.

Behind her, April heard another sound she didn't want to hear. The old church seemed to groan, and the roof gave way. All of it. And it came crashing down.

Oh, God.

It was falling on them. If they didn't do something fast, they'd be crushed.

Chase latched on to her and started running. Not toward the cruiser since it would mean literally running out in the open where there was heavy gunfire. Still using the steps for cover, he took her toward the side of the church.

To the cemetery.

And he pulled her behind the first headstone they

reached. Chase didn't stop there. He pushed her to the ground and crawled on top of her, protecting her with his body.

None of the headstones in the cemetery were that large, but at least this one was marble, and she prayed it would be enough to stop bullets.

Especially since the bullets started to come right at them.

April couldn't see much because of her position, but she had no trouble hearing the crash. The church had collapsed. No doubt what their attackers had intended right from the beginning. This hadn't been a kidnapping attempt. But rather an attempt to murder them.

They'd nearly succeeded, and they weren't out of the woods yet. Neither were Chase's brothers and the other deputies. It sickened her to think they could all be killed because of her. Especially since April still didn't know who wanted her dead.

Or why.

"The engine won't start," Jericho called out, adding plenty of profanity to that.

Definitely not good. The unmarked cruiser was their best bet at escaping. Now they'd have to use one of the other vehicles. If they could get to them, that is.

Chase cursed, too, and it took April a moment to figure out he hadn't done that because of what Jericho had said. The angle of the shots had changed. Some were still going into the cruiser and toward the deputy's truck, but the bullets were also coming at Chase and her.

Not going into the front of the headstone, either. But rather to the side.

Where they could easily be shot.

"We have to get away from here," Chase warned her a split second before he got them moving again.

They darted behind another headstone, one that was positioned so that it would give them better cover. She hoped.

"The shooters moved the car on the road," Chase said. "They're tracking us."

It took a moment for that to sink in, and it didn't sink in well. The gunmen were closing in on them.

Chase tipped his head to the gravestone behind them. It was by far the largest one in the cemetery. "We're going there. Stay as low as you can."

She wanted to remind him to do the same, but there wasn't any time. Chase took hold of her hand again, and as he fired off a shot in the direction of the gunmen, they ran, diving behind the large headstone.

But before April even hit the ground, she screamed.

Because she tripped over something.

A body.

CHASE HADN'T SEEN the body before April and he had scrambled behind the large tombstone. But he certainly saw it now.

A man on the ground.

Every drop of color vanished from April's face, and she clamped her hand over her mouth, no doubt to stop herself from screaming again. She scurried away from the body, backing up against the marble headstone.

It took April a couple of seconds to lower her hand. "Is it Quentin?" she asked, her breath gusting.

Hell, Chase hoped not.

But it was a valid question and hard to tell since it appeared the guy had been shot at point-blank range in the head. There was blood. Lots of it. It had covered much of his hair, and since the man was facedown, the only way Chase could be sure was to turn the body.

Chase reached to do that, but the shots came at them again. Thankfully, the bullets were all slamming into the marble, and this particular headstone was wide enough that it should be able to stop April and him from being shot.

Not the same for his brothers and the deputies, though.

Jericho and the others were still out there in the line of fire with a disabled vehicle. Maybe they'd managed to find some kind of cover. Or better yet, perhaps they were close to ending this attack. There wasn't any backup to call, what with Levi and Mack at the safe house and the reserve deputy manning the sheriff's office, where they were still holding a prisoner. After all, this could be some kind of diversion to break out the man who'd killed Deanne.

But it didn't feel like a diversion.

April and he were almost certainly the targets.

He fired glances all around him. The car with the gunmen was obviously still out there on the road. No one was inside the collapsed church to his right, or if they were inside, they were dead and therefore no threat.

That left the pasture to his left and behind him. Both were dotted with a few trees and some high grass. Not the easiest way for an attacker to approach them, but it was possible. That's why he had to keep watch, and April would have to help him.

Chase motioned toward the left pasture. "Make sure no one comes at us from there."

She gave a shaky nod, pinned her attention in that

direction, with the occasional glances at the body. He hated she had to see that, but they had to stay put for now.

When the angle of the bullets didn't change and come at them, Chase risked turning the body. Again, not easy. Whoever it was, he was literally dead weight, and even after Chase maneuvered him to his back, it still took him a second to recognize the guy. Not Quentin.

Shane.

April's breath rushed out again, but this time he thought maybe there was some relief in it. He was relieved, too. He wasn't a fan of Quentin's, but Chase hadn't wanted April to see him like this, either.

"Why was Shane here?" she asked.

Chase didn't have an answer for that. This was the last place he'd expected to see Renée's estranged husband, and judging from the pool of blood around him, he'd been dead for at least a couple of hours.

Dexter had checked the cemetery earlier, but Chase doubted he'd gone from grave to grave since it would have been easy to see something lurking behind a tombstone. But then, Dexter wouldn't have been looking for someone lying flat on the ground.

His phone rang, and since Chase didn't want to take his attention off their surroundings, he passed the phone to April. "It's Jericho," she relayed to him when she glanced at the screen.

"Don't put it on speaker," Chase warned her. "There could be a listening device planted on Shane's body."

Judging from the way her eyes widened, she hadn't thought of that. Considering everything else their attacker had done to get to them, Chase figured anything was a possibility, including more explosives.

April put the phone next to his ear so they both could hear, and she hit the answer button.

"Where are you?" Jericho immediately asked.

"Behind the Millers' tombstone. We found a body here. It's Shane, and it looks as if he's been dead for a while."

Jericho cursed. "Please tell me it was suicide."

"No, he was shot in the back of the head. I'm guessing he knew his killer because the person managed to get close to him."

Of course, that meant it could be any of their suspects since Shane knew all three of them. Renée would have been the one who could get the nearest to him, but Shane also knew Quentin and Malcolm.

"We haven't been able to shoot any of the gunmen," Jericho went on. "They're using rifles with scopes and are out of range. I called the Rangers, but it'll take them too long to get here. The gunmen keep moving closer."

Chase made a quick glance to verify that. His heart slammed against his chest. Because it was true. It wouldn't be long before they were in position to blast April and him to smithereens.

"We can't wait for the Rangers," Jericho explained. "We'll have to use the truck to get April and you out of there."

"I'm listening." And he hoped Jericho had a workable plan because Chase certainly didn't.

"Dexter's going to try to get the truck out to you. I'll run some interference."

"How?" Because Chase didn't want his brother rushing out in the line of fire to create a diversion.

"There are some flares in the disabled cruiser. I'll

fire them at the gunmen when Dexter's driving the truck to you."

Chase doubted the flares would do any actual damage, but they could be a distraction. Plus, flares had been known to catch fire from time to time. Maybe they'd get a lucky break and that would happen now.

"There's no easy path for Dexter to get to you," Jericho went on. He was right. The tombstones were staggered, and there definitely wasn't enough room for a truck to drive around them. "So Dexter will get as close as he can, and you'll need to make a run for it. All right?"

Chase looked at April, and he could see the fear in her eyes. Not just fear for the gunmen, but also because this plan was risky. A lot of people could be hurt or killed. But that could happen if they stayed put, too.

She nodded.

"Go for it," Chase relayed to his brother. "When the truck's in place, we'll be ready to move."

April pressed the end call button and slipped the phone back into his pocket. Now all they could do was wait, and thankfully it didn't take long for Chase to hear the truck engine.

And the shots that were now going right at the truck.

He figured Dexter was staying as low in the seat as possible, but it might not be low enough.

The truck soon came into view, and though he couldn't actually see Dexter because of the cracked side window, the deputy stopped in between the fallen church and the edge of the cemetery. There was no fence, just the distance they'd have to cover since there were three tombstones between them and the truck.

Dexter eased open the truck door, and because this plan would mean April and Chase literally diving inside, Dexter got out from behind the wheel, dropping to the floor in front of the passenger's seat to give them as much room as possible. The trick would be to get April in there first without either of them getting shot. Then, Chase could drive away, provided the gunmen hadn't disabled the tires by then.

That's where they were aiming now.

There was a swooshing sound, and Chase saw the flare shoot through the air. Jericho had a good aim because it crashed directly into the gunmen's car.

"Let's go," Chase told April.

He took hold of her hand and hauled her to her feet. However, she didn't stay there.

There was another sound. The sickening thud of a bullet hitting something. Or rather someone.

The shot slammed right into April.

Chapter Eighteen

April froze.

The scream wedged there in her throat, cutting off the air. Strangling her. She couldn't move, couldn't run, but she could feel the pain radiate from her chest and knife through her entire body. She slumped to the ground, unable to break her fall.

God, she'd been shot.

"April's been hit!" Chase yelled to someone. Maybe to his brother or Dexter.

The pain made it hard to focus, but she heard another round of gunfire. Closer than the other shots. These were coming from Chase. And from someone else. Those shots stopped after just a few seconds, but the other ones, the ones aimed at the truck, continued.

Chase dropped to his knees next to her. He ripped open her shirt. Right where the pain was the worst.

"You're okay," he said. Though his expression said otherwise. "The bullet hit the Kevlar vest."

Only then did April remember she was even wearing the vest. It'd saved her, but it certainly hadn't stopped the pain. It felt as if a heavyweight had punched her in the chest and then burned her.

"Just try to breathe," Chase instructed, his gaze firing all around them.

Easier said than done. The pain from a real gunshot wound had to be much, much worse, but April couldn't imagine it.

"Who shot me?" she managed to ask.

"A guy who sneaked into the back pasture. I got a look at his face but didn't recognize him." He flicked away the hot slug that was imbedded into the vest. "Don't worry about him, though. He's dead."

No doubt because Chase had shot him.

Good. Considering there was another body just inches from her, it should have turned her stomach to know someone else was dead, but one less hired thug increased their chances of getting out of this.

Chase's phone rang again, and he answered it without taking his attention off their surroundings. Even though he was hovering right over her, she couldn't hear what the caller said, but she could tell it wasn't good news because Chase's forehead bunched up.

"Let me see if I can move her," Chase finally said.

"What happened?" April asked the moment he finished the call.

"The gunmen shot out the truck tires. And Jericho spotted another vehicle on the road. Maybe an innocent bystander, but it could be more gunmen."

Or the person behind all of this.

All of their suspects had reasons for wanting her dead, and that might mean the person wanted to personally kill her. Of course, the shot to the vest had come darn close to doing that. If it'd been just a few inches higher, the bullet would have hit her in the neck.

"Jericho lost sight of the second car so it could be anywhere by now," Chase added.

That didn't help her regain any of her breath. "So, what do we do?" But April was almost afraid to hear the answer.

"When I give Jericho a signal that you can move, he'll shoot off more of those flares while we run to the front of the truck. We can use it for cover, and then Dexter will maneuver the truck as best he can so that you and I can head behind the rubble of the church."

April lifted her head to get an idea of how much time it would take to do that. Just a few seconds. But they'd no doubt be long, dangerous seconds. At least the rubble pile was high enough to give them some protection, and they could maybe even use the debris for cover if the gunmen changed positions again.

"What about the other car on the road?" she asked. "What if the driver comes to the back of the church, too?"

"It's a chance we have to take." He paused. "The gunmen in that black car are moving closer to the cemetery."

And closer to Chase and her.

"The Rangers are about twenty minutes out," Chase added. "We won't have to hold up much longer. Can you run?" he pressed.

April nodded, prayed it was true, and she fought the pain to get into a crouching position.

"Stay by my side," Chase instructed. "Run as fast as you can."

She gave him another nod, and Chase tossed out a rock. Probably his cue for Jericho to set off the flare because almost immediately she heard the same swooshing sound. Not one but two.

And Chase and she ran.

Even though April was nowhere near 100 percent, Chase made up for that by hooking his arm around her waist. They barreled past the trio of headstones that were between them and the truck.

The shots came at them, of course, but they pelted into the ground, kicking up dirt. That's when April got a glimpse of the reddish-colored smoke from the flare. It had created a filmy curtain between them and the shooters.

When they reached the front of the truck, Chase pulled her to the ground. They wouldn't be able to stay there long because once the smoke cleared, the gunmen would be able to shoot under the truck.

"You ready?" Dexter called out.

"Do it," Chase answered.

Dexter threw the truck into Reverse, and even though all four tires were indeed completely flat, he somehow managed to back up a couple of inches. Then forward again. Angling the truck to give them the most cover before he scrambled out of the cab and joined them on the ground.

Another flare went off.

Chase didn't waste a second. He got her moving to the debris with Dexter racing along behind them.

Thankfully, there'd been no fire from the explosion, and with the roof fully collapsed, there was nothing to fall on them. However, the debris didn't look that steady, but maybe it would hold up until they could get out of there.

They ducked behind the first pile of rubble. It was mainly what was left of an office. Books, chairs and a broken desk stuck out from the chunks of the roof that had demolished it.

"Damn," Chase said. He leaned out and fired a shot.

"The men moved the car right by the truck," Dexter explained to her since she couldn't see. She was on Chase's left side with Dexter behind her.

April soon got proof that the gunmen were closing in because the shots came right at them. Again. She glanced at Chase to see if he was about to tell them to move, but he was focused on returning fire.

There was a thudding sound behind her, and April whirled around to see what had happened.

No!

Dexter was on the ground.

Before April could even react, someone knocked her gun from her hand and grabbed her.

CHASE SAW THE movement from the corner of his eye and pivoted toward April and Dexter.

His heart went to his knees.

Dexter was down. Not shot. It appeared that someone had clubbed him on the head and he was unconscious. The someone was wearing a ski mask like the other gunmen and now had April. She was fighting to get loose.

And the person—a man—was trying to shoot her.

Chase lunged at them, sending all three of them to the ground. The man slung his elbow into Chase's jaw, hitting him so hard that the pain exploded in his head. He fought off the pain and tried to latch on to April to pull her away. It was the only option he had right now because Chase didn't have a clean shot.

April was no doubt still reeling from taking a slug to the chest, but that didn't stop her from fighting. She clawed and kicked at him. Chase tossed his gun aside so he could go after the guy's own weapon. Because of all the flailing around, he only managed to take hold of the man's right wrist, but maybe that would be enough to stop him from aiming at April again.

Something he was clearly trying to do.

"Move away if you can," Chase told her.

She tried to do just that, but the man hooked his arm around her neck and put her in a choke hold. Not good. Because as long as April was in the middle of this, there was a chance she could be shot. Or strangled to death. Her attacker was trying to do both.

Chase tried to bash the man's hand against the ground and managed a few hits. Not enough, though, to dislodge the gun from his grip. Whoever this was, he was fighting like a wild animal.

April made a strangled sound and tried to pry his grip off her throat. The guy held on. Tightening the choke hold.

He was killing her right in front of Chase.

It was a risk, but Chase took one of his hands off the man's shooting wrist so he could punch him. Hard. Not easy to do, though, with April in the way. Still, he managed one good hit.

But then the shot blasted from the gun.

The man had managed to pull the trigger.

So many bad thoughts went through Chase's head. Had April been shot? She stopped struggling, her hands going to her ears, and for several terrifying seconds, Chase thought maybe the bullet had gone into her head.

But no blood, thank God.

The shot had been so close to her that it'd no doubt caused a jarring pain. The sound was clanging in Chase's ears, too, but he forced himself to keep fighting. Unfortunately, the guy did the same thing.

Chase pinned the man's right hand, and the gun, to the ground and tried to push April out of the way.

Another shot.

Hell.

Chase didn't know where the bullets were going, but Dexter was right there just a yard or so away, and the shots could hit him. Plus, they had an even bigger problem. He couldn't check to see where that black car was, but Chase figured the car, and all the gunmen inside it, were making their way to them so they could help their fellow thug. Once that happened, Chase would be seriously outgunned until Jericho and the others could get back, too.

April pulled her hands from her ears, and even though she was clearly still in pain, she started to fight back again. Both a blessing and a curse. He didn't want her just to give in to this, but he would have preferred that she get as far away from that gun as possible.

"Kill them both!" the man yelled.

Chase had no trouble recognizing that voice. And it wasn't the voice of just another hired gun.

It was Malcolm.

April froze for a second. They'd both known Malcolm was a suspect, of course, but Chase hadn't expected him to be directly involved in this since all the other attacks had come from hired guns.

More shots came, smacking into the ground all around them. Obviously, the men in that black car were now in a position to do some damage and to carry out their boss's order.

Kill them both.

Chase tried to make sure that didn't happen. He dropped onto his back, lifted Malcolm's wrist and gun, and he fired at the thugs who were shooting around them. He had no idea where the bullet went, but Chase hoped it would get them to back off so he could take care of this idiot who was trying to murder April.

Malcolm ripped off his mask and then yanked April back into his grip. Managed, too, to put her in another choke hold. More than ready to put an end to this, Chase punched him again. And again. He would have delivered a third punch if a bullet hadn't sliced across the top of shoulder.

The pain was searing and roared through him. Chase knew it wasn't a fatal shot, but it slowed him down just enough that Malcolm shoved Chase off him.

And Malcolm put the gun to April's head.

No. This couldn't be happening. After everything they'd been through, and survived, he couldn't let Malcolm kill her.

Chase snatched up his gun and scrambled to the side of some of the debris. He took aim. But like before, he didn't have a shot. Not with Malcolm holding April in front of him that way.

"You've been hit," April said, her attention not on fighting for her life but rather on his bloody shoulder.

"He'll be dead if he doesn't back off," Malcolm snarled. "April, if you want your boyfriend to live, tell him to stop and put down his gun. I hadn't planned on killing him, but if he gets in the way, I'll do just that."

"Please stop," she told Chase without hesitation.

Chase had no intention of stopping, but he wasn't sure how to get her out of this. He glanced over his shoulder. The black car was only about ten yards away, and even though Jericho and the others were shooting at it, the vehicle was inching closer, like a jungle cat ready to attack. Worse, it wouldn't be long before the men in that car would be able to use the debris for cover, too.

"I don't want you to die," April added to Chase. "So, please, just let Malcolm take me."

"Malcolm will kill you," he reminded her. "He wants to punish you for Tina's murder."

"Because she deserves to be punished," Malcolm readily admitted.

So, that was indeed his motive. Not that it did them any good to hear it spelled out. Still, he might be able to use it to bargain with Malcolm.

"Tina was a good cop," Chase reminded him. "She wouldn't have approved of any of this."

Malcolm's eyes narrowed. "You don't know that. She was gunned down trying to do her job. I doubt she'd shed any tears over the death of a lowlife like Crossman."

"You had him killed?" Chase asked.

Chase already knew the answer, but he got confirmation of it anyway when Malcolm nodded. But the man didn't just nod. He motioned toward his hired thugs in the car.

"And I figure Tina would be pleased that I'm avenging her death," Malcolm added.

It was hard to reason with a man obsessed with revenge, but Chase had to figure out something.

April's eyes widened, and even though Chase figured he wasn't going to like what he saw, he glanced over his shoulder again.

And, no, he didn't like it.

Two ski-masked gunmen were out of the car. Not alone.

They had a hostage.

Chapter Nineteen

Renée.

April certainly hadn't forgotten about the woman, but she was surprised to see that Renée was on the business end of a gun rather than the one who was pulling the trigger.

Maybe this was some kind of ruse.

Though April couldn't imagine why the woman would pretend to be a hostage. Still, it was hard to figure out the motives of someone so mentally unstable.

"You shot Shane!" Renée shouted, her attention zooming straight to Malcolm. "Is he dead?"

"He's dead," April confirmed.

Renée screamed and started struggling, trying to get away from her captors. It didn't work. The men held on to her, and when she didn't stop fighting to break free, one of them punched her right in the face. Hard. Renée's head flopped back, and blood splattered from what looked to be a broken nose.

Apparently, the woman wasn't a fake hostage after all. Or if she was, this was a convincing act.

One of the men continued to keep Renée in a fierce grip, and the other hurried to Dexter. The deputy was still unconscious, but the thug put some plastic cuffs on him and kicked Dexter's gun away.

While they were occupied with that, April tried to elbow Malcolm in the stomach so she could try to break free. She failed, and Malcolm tightened his grip on her even more.

Malcolm tipped his head to Dexter and then glanced at the thug who was hovering over him. "Shoot the deputy in the head if Chase doesn't drop his gun right now." His voice was ice cold.

April saw the debate in Chase's eyes. A very short one. Because they both knew the man would indeed murder Dexter.

Chase tossed his gun to the ground.

Her heart sank. Of course, April already knew they were in extreme danger, but now neither of them was armed. And they were outnumbered. Plus, Chase was hurt. The blood from the shot to his shoulder was now on the front of his shirt. It didn't look as if he would bleed out, but he needed medical attention. Fast. For that to happen, they had to get out of this.

"Go ahead and kill Renée if she doesn't stop fighting," Malcolm told his men. "I'd wanted them all together for this, but I can always change the plan."

What the heck was going on here?

"Why would you want Renée dead?" April asked.

"She's a loose end," Chase provided when Malcolm didn't say anything. "I figure Malcolm hired the hacker to get into WITSEC files but couldn't find Quentin because he wasn't where he was supposed to be. Malcolm then convinced Renée to kidnap Bailey so he could use the baby to draw Quentin out."

"The plan worked," Malcolm said. "Well, nearly. I'd

wanted Quentin to take the blame for all of this, but now that you've seen my face, that's not going to happen. Still, you can save your brothers and the other lawmen."

"How?" But Chase didn't wait for an answer. "By agreeing to let you leave with April, Renée and me?"

But they wouldn't be just leaving with Malcolm. He would kill them all when he had the rest of his so-called plan in place. That meant he wanted to get Quentin, too, and would likely use her—and possibly even Renée—to lure Quentin into a trap.

A trap that just might work.

"Come on," Malcolm said, and he started moving her.

Malcolm didn't take her toward the black car but to the other side of what remained of the church. Jericho had mentioned something about another vehicle, and it was possible Malcolm planned to use that to escape with them so he could finish out his plan.

"I'm not going anywhere with you," Renée shouted. "You killed Shane." A hoarse sob tore from her mouth, and she was obviously in pain from the punch to the face because she was wincing. "Why would you do that?"

"Sorry, but Shane was another loose end." That's the only explanation Malcolm gave them.

Though April could fill in the blanks. Shane loved Renée, and he had been a bulldog trying to track her down. Malcolm must have known Shane wouldn't give up. Something Malcolm would have totally understood since he was doing the same thing to get justice for Tina.

"Want to save your brothers?" Malcolm repeated to Chase. "If so, yell for them to put down their guns. They won't be hurt."

"And I'm supposed to believe that?" Chase challenged. "You've killed Shane, Crossman, Deanne—"

"Deanne was a mistake," Malcolm snapped. Not exactly an ice-cold voice now. There was some anger in it, too. "That was Renée's doing, wasn't it?"

There was more sobbing from Renée. "It was an accident. No one was supposed to die. The man I hired panicked when he spotted Chase."

"Well, someone did die." Malcolm sounded so angry that April thought he might shoot Renée then and there. "You had only one thing to do. Use the baby to draw out Quentin, and instead you got Deanne killed. She was Tina's CI, and they were close. You'll pay for that, bitch."

So, that explained why Renée's head was on the chopping block. Malcolm was trying to take care of anyone who'd wronged Tina or him.

April glanced back at Malcolm. "I can't believe you trusted Renée with my daughter."

"Nothing was supposed to happen to the baby. I warned Renée of that right from the start. I liked Bailey. In fact, the only reason I didn't gun you down when I first saw you in the hospital was because of her. I didn't want you shot in front of her."

Sweet heaven. He'd been planning to kill her even then. And April wouldn't have seen it coming. She'd been so torn up about Bailey's premature birth that she hadn't realized the danger was so close to her.

Too bad. Or maybe she could have ended it before it got this far.

There was more gunfire. All of it came from the front of what was left of the church. Probably more hired guns taking shots at Jericho and the others. She prayed they'd be able to stay out of harm's way, especially since she might not be able to save Chase.

That broke her heart.

He could die here. And all because of her. April wished she could go back and undo the damage, but instead more people, including Chase, could keep paying for the mistake she'd made. Malcolm would almost certainly kill both of them once he had this plan finalized.

And that meant Bailey would be an orphan.

April felt the tears spill onto her cheek. Then, she felt something else. Something much, much stronger.

The rage bubbling inside her.

She was letting Malcolm drag her to her death, and that was about to end. If she was going to die anyway, she'd do it fighting. April used that rage, pinpointing it into her fist. She whirled around and punched Malcolm as hard as she could.

Malcolm staggered back. Just a little. Just enough to off-balance him. She knocked the gun from his hand as Chase tackled the man. They both went crashing into the debris, some of it falling on them.

April knew she couldn't just stand there and watch. She snatched up Chase's gun, and she fired at the gunman standing over Dexter. She wasn't sure who was more surprised—him or her—when the bullet hit him right squarely in the chest. He collapsed onto the ground before he could even get off a shot.

Renée screamed again, and April pivoted in that direction, ready to stop the second gunman. But Renée was clawing at the man's face, and she kneed him in the groin. Again. And again.

The gunman fired, but his shot went into the dirt. So did he, and he howled in pain while Renée just kept kicking him.

"Get his gun," April told the woman.

Renée did that, after she kicked him again. She ripped

the gun from his hand, shot him in the stomach before she whirled around, her gaze landing on Malcolm. No scream this time. Just a low feral sound fueled by her rage. Considering that her face was streaked with blood and her nostrils were flaring, April doubted the woman had any control left.

And that meant Renée could possibly shoot Chase while she was gunning for Malcolm.

She raced toward Renée, to try to latch on to the gun. But again, she was too late. Screaming, Renée pulled the trigger.

April could have sworn her heart stopped. Her breath certainly did. It stalled there in her lungs, and it seemed to take an eternity for her to get to Chase and pull him away from Malcolm.

There was so much blood.

Too much.

"Chase," she managed to say. "Don't die. Please don't."

He shook his head. "It's not my blood. Well, most of it anyway."

It took April a moment to fight through the panic and realize he was right. Chase's shoulder was still bleeding, but it was nothing compared with the blood on Malcolm's chest.

Renée had shot him.

Chase took April by the arm, maneuvering her away from Malcolm. In the same motion, he yanked the gun from Renée's hand.

"I hit him," Renée said. "I hope I killed him."

Not yet. Malcolm was still alive, his eyes open, but he wasn't moving, and he was losing way too much blood to stay alive for long.

April saw the movement from the corner of her eye

and pivoted in that direction. It was Jax and Jericho. Thank God. And they had their attention focused on that other car. The one that no doubt contained other gunmen ready to do Malcolm's bidding.

"I hope you burn in hell for murdering Shane," Renée said, spitting on Malcolm.

April held her back. Not because she thought Malcolm deserved to stay alive for even a second longer, but because he appeared to be trying to say something to Chase.

"Two out of three's not bad," Malcolm mumbled, his voice weak, and the life draining out of his eyes.

"What do you mean?" Chase asked.

"I got Crossman." Malcolm lifted his gaze to April. "And while you and Chase might walk away from this, your brother won't. Quentin's a dead man." He lifted his hand, the same gesture he'd used with the other gunmen. It stayed in the air just a second before it slumped to the ground.

Malcolm didn't draw another breath.

Almost instantly, the door to the other car opened, and Quentin stepped out. Alive. But she soon realized what Malcolm had meant when he said her brother was a dead man. There was another of Malcolm's hired killers behind Quentin, and he had a gun pointed at Quentin's head.

"Tell your brother goodbye," the man taunted. "Because you're about to see him die right before your eyes."

This wasn't a bluff. She felt that in every part of her body. Quentin obviously did, too. He wasn't fighting. He'd already surrendered.

"Give me the gun," Chase said to April.

She handed it to him, not sure what Chase had in mind. And she didn't have to wait long to find out, either.

Without warning, Chase lifted the gun and fired. Not

a head shot. Probably because he would have hit Quentin. Instead, Chase shot the gunman in the leg.

The guy howled in pain. Staggered back a step. Just enough for Chase to shoot him again. The bullet smacked into his shoulder and put the gunman on his knees.

Quentin didn't waste any time grabbing the man's gun, and he turned, aiming the weapon at him. For a moment, April thought Quentin would shoot the man in cold blood. But Quentin cursed, lowered the gun and started toward them.

The relief flooded through her. But it didn't last. Because she looked at Chase and saw something she didn't want to see. More blood. The front of his shirt was red now, and choking back a sound of pain, he leaned against her.

"Call an ambulance," April shouted, and she caught on to Chase a split second before he lost consciousness.

Chapter Twenty

Chase opened his eyes. And he groaned. What he wanted to do was curse, but the first person he saw was April, and she had worry written all over her face. It was on Jax's and Jericho's faces, too, and Chase was responsible for it being there.

"I'm all right," Chase insisted, and he sat up. Or rather that's what he tried to do, but that's when he realized he was in a hospital bed and hooked up to an IV. He also realized he was in pain.

What the heck?

He remembered getting shot, of course. Hard to forget that, especially now with the blistering pain. He also remembered being in an ambulance, but everything was a little fuzzy after that.

"You're not all right," April said. Oh, man. She'd been crying and was still blinking back tears. "You had surgery to remove the bullet from your shoulder, and lost a lot of blood."

Jericho looked down at him. "He's fine. Chase is used to getting shot and stabbed, aren't you, little brother?"

That was a bad joke. But also true. He had been shot and stabbed before. Chase appreciated his brother's attempt at humor because it lightened his mood a little. However, it didn't work for April.

She went closer, eased down on the edge of the bed next to him. "You could have been killed."

He hated seeing her cry or hearing her voice break. It crushed his heart six ways to Sunday. And that's why he pulled her down for a kiss. Chase figured they both could use it, and he was right, though he wasn't sure how his brothers would react to the kiss.

Nor did he care.

There was a cut on April's head, and he moved away her hair so he could see it better. That set off a new wave of rage inside him. Malcolm had been responsible for that. Responsible, too, for nearly getting them all killed.

"Where's Bailey?" he asked.

"In the hall. Levi and Mack brought her from the safe house and your mother has her. Your mom will bring her in to see you in a few minutes. I just wanted to make sure you were up to it first."

Chase didn't even have to think about that. "I'm definitely up to it."

Like the kiss, seeing Bailey was something he needed, though he was certain his mom was enjoying every second of holding her first and only granddaughter.

"How's everyone else?" Chase asked. "Was Dexter or Quentin hurt?"

All three of them shook their heads. "Shaken up but okay," Jax continued. "Dexter's got a concussion from the blow to the head, but he'll be fine." He paused, his gaze drifting to April.

"Quentin's in a holding cell," April finished for him. "He'll be charged with faking his kidnapping."

"Jail time?" Chase added.

Jericho shrugged. "Some. If he had a clean record, maybe not, but this isn't his first rodeo."

"Jail time might do him some good," April snarled. "Even Quentin agrees with that, and if he hadn't, it wouldn't have mattered. I'm not bailing him out."

Good. Because Quentin had to grow up eventually, and even if he didn't, it was obvious that April was going to make her brother stand on his own two feet.

"Please tell me Malcolm's really dead." Because Chase hoped that wasn't something he'd dreamed.

"He's dead," Jax verified. "And Gene Rooks has decided that now that his boss is dead, he'll talk to get a few of the charges off the table. Rooks told us that Malcolm had explosives planted under the church when he found out that's where Deanne's funeral would be. Malcolm was guessing April might show up."

And she had. All because they'd wanted to set a trap. A trap that backfired big-time.

"When the explosives didn't work," Chase said, "then he turned his hired guns on all of us."

Chase cursed again, and April leaned in, stared at him. "This wasn't your fault. Or even mine. I know that now. If Malcolm hadn't come after us at the church, he would have found another way. Maybe a way that would have involved Bailey."

She was right. Malcolm was rich and willing to do anything to get revenge for Tina's murder. Since he'd found someone willing to hack into WITSEC files before, he likely would have tried it again and again until he found April and him. And Bailey would have indeed been with them.

"You're being logical about this," Chase pointed out to her.

April shook her head, blinked back more tears. "Not logical. Just thankful we're all alive."

Yeah, he was right there with her, and Chase wished he could have a moment alone, to tell her things. And kiss her.

Mercy, he wanted to kiss her.

But judging from Jax's and Jericho's expressions, there was still more they had to say. "Renée didn't escape again, did she?" Chase asked.

"No," Jericho jumped to answer. Now there was something more than concern for him on his brother's face. There was relief. "She's in custody, and after her hearing she'll be taken to the mental hospital. With all the charges against her, she'll be there a long time."

More good news. Not that Chase thought Renée would come after them, but she needed some serious help. "Did Renée say how she knew that Malcolm had shot Shane?"

Jax nodded. "Renée's been as chatty as Rooks. Malcolm lured her to a meeting near the church. He told her that Quentin wanted to see her. She didn't trust Malcolm so she called Shane to go with her. Malcolm shot Shane and then kidnapped Renée."

So Malcolm could no doubt set her up to take the blame for April's and Quentin's murders. And his plan might have worked if April and he had been killed in the explosion. Then, the gunmen could have picked off Quentin, too. That would have left a mentally unstable Renée holding the bag.

"I don't suppose Rooks or Renée knew anything about Crossman's murder?" Chase asked.

"No," Jericho verified. "The prison warden will investigate, of course, but I'm betting he won't get any confessions."

Probably not. Malcolm had paid someone to murder Crossman, but he'd also probably covered the money trail so that it couldn't be traced back to him. Since Malcolm had been at the prison that same day, it was even possible he'd managed to slip someone cash to shank Crossman.

"With Crossman dead and Malcolm dead, there's no reason for us to go to WITSEC," April said, caution in her voice. "Right?"

"Right," Chase assured her. Of course, that left them both with a really big question.

What next?

Chase didn't have much time to consider that because there was a light tap on the door, and when it opened a few inches, his mom peeked in. Smiling. At first, but then she got that worried look everyone had when he'd first woken up.

"I must look pretty bad," Chase told her, "but it's okay. I'm fine."

And he was, and that fine part went up a significant notch when his mother stepped into the room and Chase saw she had Bailey in her arms. The baby was wide awake and looking very content to have her grandmother holding her.

"I brought you a visitor," his mother said, coming closer to the bed.

April kissed Bailey, and his mom leaned in to put Bailey into the crook of his good arm. Bailey looked up at him, and she smiled.

Now, that was a cure for pain and just about anything else.

"She's such a good baby," his mother announced. "I hope I get to spend lots of time with her after you move April and her to the ranch." She paused, froze as if she'd said the wrong thing. "Sorry, I guess that's something you two probably need to talk about."

It was, and his brothers picked up on that right away. Jericho took out his phone and mumbled something about needing to check on a few things. Jax suddenly wanted to get home to see his son.

"Why don't I wait in the hall for a little while," his mother added. "Want me to take the baby with me?"

Something else Chase didn't have to think about. "No. Leave her here." He wasn't ready to let go of Bailey just yet, even though it would be harder to kiss April with the baby in his arms.

Or not.

April proved him wrong because the moment his mother stepped out of the room, April kissed him. No logistics problems at all, and it wasn't as if he was in any shape to haul April off to bed anyway.

Soon, though, maybe he could remedy that. Maybe he could remedy a lot of things.

"I want Bailey and you to move in with me," he tossed out there. Not that it was a surprise offer since his mom had already suggested it. And Chase waited. Breath held. Because what April said next would be some of the most important words he'd ever hear.

"Are you sure you want that?" she asked.

Well, it wasn't the enthusiastic response Chase had hoped for, but he was certain of the answer. "Absolutely. The danger's over, and there's no reason you two can't be there. Is there?" he added when April's forehead bunched up.

She didn't say anything for several really long moments. "But are you sure it's what *you* want?" It was nearly the same words, but he picked up on the under-current of her question.

"I want you there." Chase managed to maneuver her closer so he could kiss her again. "I want *you*."

When he eased back from her, he saw relief, but it wasn't relief he was going for. "We have a beautiful daughter," he reminded her. "She's perfect, but I think we can build on perfect."

Again, he waited, but April's forehead only bunched up even more. "I'm in love with you," she blurted out. "There, I said it, and I don't want to unsay it, either. I love you and I don't want to just move in with you, I want—"

He kissed her again. Hard and long. Hopefully enough for her to realize it wasn't necessary for her to defend her love for him or the life she wanted together with Bailey and him.

Because Chase wanted the same thing.

The kiss left her a little breathless, Him, too. And it left him wanting a whole lot more.

"I want it all, too," he told her. "You, the baby…the home. Together. Oh, and I want you to marry me."

He hadn't meant to make that sound like an after-thought. It wasn't. It was something he'd been think-ing about since he'd come too darn close to losing April today. That ordeal hadn't made him fall in love with her, but it'd been the knock upside his head to make him re-alize it.

Tears came back to her eyes. Then, a smile. "You're proposing?"

"You bet I am. I would get down on one knee, but I'm not exactly in any shape to do that. Just use your imagi-nation and imagine that I'm on one knee."

April smiled. "I'm imagining a lot of things when it comes to you."

So was Chase. And he couldn't wait to get started on all of it.

Bailey squirmed, kicked at him as if reminding him she was a part of this, too. "I just asked your mom to marry me. What do you think she'll say?"

Bailey smiled.

"That's the right answer," April said, kissing Bailey. Then, Chase. And then April made the moment perfect with just one word.

"Yes."

* * * * *

Look for more books in USA TODAY
*bestselling author Delores Fossen's
Harlequin Intrigue miniseries*
APPALOOSA PASS RANCH *later this year.
And be sure to also check out her HQN Books trilogy,*
THE McCORD BROTHERS!

SPECIAL EXCERPT FROM

H HARLEQUIN®

I N T R I G U E

*The cries of an abandoned baby force a by-the-book
Kansas City lawman and a free-spirited social worker
to join forces and protect the newborn. But what
happens when their lives are also put in jeopardy?*

Read on for a sneak preview of
APB: BABY,
which launches USA TODAY *bestselling author*
Julie Miller's brand-new miniseries,
THE PRECINCT: BACHELORS IN BLUE.

Her gaze darted up to meet his, and he felt her skin warming
beneath his touch before she turned her hand to squeeze
his fingers. Then she pulled away to finish packing. "But
we've already been too much of an imposition. You need
to go by St. Luke's to visit your grandfather and spend
time with your family. I've already kept you from them
longer than you planned this morning. I can grab the car
seat and call a cab so you don't even have to drive us.
Tommy and I will be fine—as long as you don't mind us
staying in your apartment. Maintenance said there was a
chance they could get someone to see to my locks today."

"And they also said it could be Monday morning." No.
Tommy needed Dr. Niall Watson of the KCPD Crime Lab
to be his friend right now. And no matter how independent
she claimed to be, Lucy needed a friend, too. Right now
that friend was going to be him. Niall shrugged into
his black KCPD jacket and picked up the sweater coat

she'd draped over the back of her chair. "I work quickly and methodically, Lucy. I will find the answers you and Tommy need. But I can't do that when I'm not able to focus. And having half the city between you and me when we don't know what all this means or if you and Tommy are in any kind of danger—"

"Are you saying I'm a distraction?"

Nothing but. Confused about whether that was some type of flirtatious remark or whether she was simply seeking clarification, Niall chose not to answer. Instead, he handed her the sweater and picked up Tommy in his carrier. "Get his things and let's go."

Don't miss APB: BABY
by USA TODAY bestselling author Julie Miller,
available June 2016 wherever
Harlequin® Intrigue books and ebooks are sold.

www.Harlequin.com

Reading Has Its Rewards

Earn **FREE BOOKS!**

Register at **Harlequin My Rewards** and submit your Harlequin purchases from wherever you shop to earn points for free books and other exclusive rewards.

Plus submit your purchases from now till May 30th for a chance to win a $500 Visa Card*.

Visit **HarlequinMyRewards.com** today

Earn **FREE REWARDS** Join Today! HarlequinMyRewards.com

MYR16R1

THE WORLD IS BETTER WITH

Romance

Harlequin has everything from contemporary, passionate and heartwarming to suspenseful and inspirational stories.

Whatever your mood, we have a romance just for you!